All Hallows' Eve in Stickleback Hollow

The Mysteries of Stickleback Hollow

By C.S. Woolley

A Mightier Than the Sword UK Publication

©2017

All Hallows' Eve in Stickleback Hollow

The Mysteries of Stickleback Hollow

By C. S. Woolley

A Mightier Than the Sword UK Publication

Paperback Edition

Copyright © c. s. woolley 2017

Cover Design © c. s. woolley 2017

For

Szonja, Tom, Josh,

Carl, Callum, Dan,

Lou, Grace, Chloe, Beth,

Fraser, Jamie,

Harry and Stuart

Author's Note

Thanks for taking the time to read *All Hallows' Eve in Stickleback Hollow*, I hope you enjoy it, there is much more to come in the series if you do! This book touches on the supernatural elements and unexplained circumstances that often plague our minds on the spookiest night of the year.

The Characters

Lady Sarah Montgomery Baird Watson-Wentworth

The heroine

Brigadier General George Webb-Kneelingroach

Guardian of Lady Sarah and owner of Grangeback

Bosworth

The butler

Mrs Bosworth

The housekeeper

Cooky

The cook

Mr Alexander Hunter

A huntsman and groundskeeper of Grangeback

Constable Arwyn Evans

Policeman in Stickleback Hollow

Doctor Jack Hales

The doctor in Stickleback Hollow

Miss Angela Baker

The seamstress in Stickleback Hollow

Wilson

The innkeeper in Stickleback Hollow

Mrs Emma Wilson

Wife of Wilson and cook at the inn

Mr Henry Cartwright

Owner of Duffleton Hall

Stanley Baker

Son of Miss Baker

Lee Baker

Son of Miss Baker

Reverend Percy Butterfield

The vicar in Stickleback Hollow

Mr Richard Hales

Son of Doctor Hales

Mr Gordon Hales

Son of Doctor Hales

Mr Daniel Cooper

A gentleman from Tatton Park

Mr Harry Taylor

A gentleman from Staffordshire

Mrs Ruth Cooper

Mother of Daniel

The Honourable Mr Wilbraham Egerton

Owner of Tatton Park

Mrs Elizabeth Egerton nee Sykes

Wife of Wilbraham

Mr Wilbraham Egerton

Son of Wilbraham & Elizabeth

Mr Thomas Egerton

Son of Wilbraham & Elizabeth

Mrs Charlotte Egerton nee Milner

Wife of Thomas

Mr Edward Christopher Egerton

Son of Wilbraham & Elizabeth

Miss Mary Pierrepont

Fiancée of Edward

Miss Elizabeth Wessex

Fiancée of Harry

Lady Szonja, Countess of Huntingdon

Cousin of Elizabeth Egerton

John Smith

An Alias

Lady Carol-Ann Margaret de Mandeville, Duchess of Aumale and Montagu

The villain

Chapter 1

It is the prerogative of women to make men wait. At least that is what Lady Cynthia Watson-Wentworth had always told her daughter. Sarah didn't see the point in making anyone wait for her.

When she had lived in London, it had been the practice of her aunts and cousins to keep the men waiting for hours for them before an evening out. This seemed to be expected, as the men spent their time waiting engaged in a game of billiards, drinking something that came in short cut-crystal glasses or smoking.

Sometimes they did all three.

Once she had escaped from London to the safety of Stickleback Hollow, Sarah was certain that she wouldn't have to attend parties or events that caused women to make men wait for them – or at least here there wouldn't be many of them.

It was two weeks after she had returned from Chester with Mr Hunter, having solved the mystery of the break-in at

13

Grangeback, when the invitation arrived.

It was hand-delivered in an unassuming white envelope that masterfully hid the disagreeable contents. Bosworth was still feeling unwell and had been ordered to rest by the Brigadier, so it was one of the footmen that received the envelope.

It was addressed to:

Brigadier Webb-Kneelingroach & Lady Montgomery Baird Watson-Wentworth.

When Sarah had come back from walking to Swallow's End and back, she had found the envelope ominously staring at her from the sideboard. Aside from the people of Stickleback Hollow, the dean of Chester Cathedral and a small number of the newly formed Cheshire constabulary, no one knew she was living at Grangeback.

She had waited until the Brigadier had come home from visiting Doctor Hales before opening the envelope. It was, after all, addressed to both of them. It would have been extremely rude to open it without George.

Sarah was the ward of Brigadier George Webb-

Kneelingroach and his heiress, due to inherit the Grangeback estate. However, this wasn't common knowledge. It had only been two days since the papers had been signed, and Sarah was certain that only Mrs Bosworth, Mr Hunter and Doctor Hales knew about it.

"You open it, Sarah." George said as he sat down in the drawing room.

"It's your house, Brigadier; surely you should be the one to open it," Sarah argued.

"Nonsense, this is your home now too. Besides, it's addressed to you, and I would imagine that there haven't been too many times in your life when you've received post," George grinned as he lit his pipe.

Sarah sighed and turned over the envelope. It had been sealed with wax, and an elaborate coat-of-arms was emblazoned in the wax. She carefully peeled open the seal and pulled out a thick piece of white card that was decorated in gold leaf.

"The Honourable Wilbraham Egerton and Mrs Elizabeth Egerton cordially invite Brigadier George Webb-Kneelingroach and Lady Sarah Mary May Montgomery Baird Watson-Wentworth to attend the Tatton Park All Hallows'

Eve ball and celebrations," Sarah read the invitation, "How do people know my full name?" she asked.

"Interested parties always have ways of finding these things out," George replied as he puffed on his pipe.

"A ball and celebrations, what does that involve?" Sarah asked as she put down the invitation and sat down on one of the sofas in the room.

"It involves me dressing in my finest evening attire and you donning something outrageously difficult to fit through a double doorway. Then there is food, dancing, drinking, some form of spiritualist nonsense and feeding the poor. That's normally how they do things," George said, clearly enjoying Sarah's apparent discomfort.

"Do we have to go?" Sarah groaned.

"Of course! It is the perfect opportunity to introduce you to the wider neighbourhood. It will be quite the enjoyable evening," George insisted.

"But I don't have anything to wear," Sarah complained.

"Ha! I know you and Alex visited the dressmaker and cobbler in Chester and I know what you ordered. There will be more than enough in outrageous fashion coming to this house in the next few days for you to wear to balls for the next five years," George laughed.

"But they haven't arrived yet," Sarah replied.

"On the contrary, some of the packages arrived this afternoon, according to Mrs Bosworth. She is checking them and ensuring they are clean and pressed before they are put away in your room," George grinned.

"I'm terrible at balls," Sarah huffed and slouched on the sofa.

"I am sure you shall be your usual charming self. Besides the neighbourhood is filled with worthless young men who are just dying to throw themselves at a beautiful woman. It will make for a most entertaining evening," George didn't sound at all sympathetic.

"Will I know anyone at this ball?" Sarah asked, looking sullen.

"The doctor will be there with his two sons, and the Chief Constable is likely to be there, but other than that, there won't be," George closed his eyes as he enjoyed his pipe.

"I'm not sure the Chief Constable will be all that happy to see me," Sarah said under her breath.

"He's a man of order and justice; you are the very heart

of discord. You'll find some people to talk to though, but you shouldn't worry about impressing everyone there. Most of them you'll only see at these kinds of events, and they tend to be the type of people you want to avoid in any case," George replied.

"That doesn't exactly inspire confidence," Sarah sighed.

"Perhaps not, but it is a few weeks away yet. I am sure we shall see many people coming to the house before then to meet you," George grinned, his eyes still closed.

"Why do you say that?" Sarah asked, sitting up straight.

"Those invited will all be talking about who shall be attending. Bush telegraphs are very good in this part of the world. It will take maybe two days until everyone who is going knows your name," George puffed on his pipe.

"I thought I'd escaped this when I left London," Sarah moaned.

"Sadly, no matter where you are in England, society will find you. However, these events are few and far between. Christmas is enjoyed solely by the village, so you needn't worry about another ball until the New Year, and then the next one is at Easter. Then you have the Summer Hunt Ball and then the All Hallows' Eve ball. That is the sum total of the engagements that exist here - hardly as tiresome as the constant hither and yon of London," George said, leaning forward.

"No, it's not. And I suppose it is only for a few hours," Sarah said with resignation.

"Precisely, and who knows, you might even enjoy yourself," George grinned.

Chapter 2

Sarah went to bed that night and found she couldn't sleep. Mrs Bosworth had placed her new gowns and the shoes that had arrived for her in the wardrobe. She had looked over them before she had changed for bed and decided that the green and silver silk dress would be best.

It was a dress that had been modelled on India fashion. Sarah felt more comfortable wearing clothes similar to those that she had worn when her parents were alive, and she had lived in the province of the Empire.

The dress was designed to be worn without the heavy petticoats that most of Sarah's new dresses required. It had been made by Miss Baker in the village of Stickleback Hollow. Sarah had been surprised that Miss Baker had such rich silks to work with, but she had been delighted with the results. It reminded her of a dress her mother wore when she was a little girl.

Though the idea of attending a ball wasn't a prospect that Sarah relished, it wasn't something to keep her awake at night. Instead, it was the memory of her mother that stopped her from sleeping.

Ever since she had met with Thomas Forsythe in Chester Cathedral and discovered that her parents had not been the people she thought they were, she had struggled to sleep.

Small things brought back memories from her childhood that she lay awake questioning. The dress that she planned to wear on All Hallows' Eve had made her think of all the times her parents went out to formal events.

Sarah now wondered how many of those events had been meetings with the shadowy figure of John Smith that lurked somewhere across the sea and had been so set on acquiring the pocket watch of her father.

She had put the pocket watch back in her father's luggage that sat, still locked in her dressing room, along with the luggage that had belonged to her mother.

After lying awake for several hours, Sarah decided to go down to the stables and visit with the horse that George had bought for her.

The rest of the household was asleep as she slipped down the stairs with a candle in hand. She took the key for the backdoor off the hook in the kitchen and locked it behind her as she went out to the stables. She put the key in the pocket of her dressing gown so that she wouldn't lose it.

She hadn't thought that there was any need to dress to go down to the stables as there would be no one there to see her in the dead of night.

She had taken one of the lanterns from the kitchen and left her candle by the window. She had lit the lantern with the candle and then been sure to extinguish it before leaving the house.

It was unwise to leave an unattended candle burning, especially when the rest of the house was asleep.

Sarah walked slowly down to the stables. The night air was cold. It was the beginning of autumn, but she hadn't been in England very long and still hadn't adjusted to the temperatures being much cooler than they were in India.

She pulled her dressing gown tightly around her to try and keep out most of the cold. It was much warmer in the stables than outside. There were a few horses that belonged to the Grangeback estate; most were horses that were used to pull carriages and traps, but there were two beautiful horses that George had bought for riding.

22

They were both Friesian horses, and the closest breed to the destriers that the kings of old had ridden into battle. George bought a black stallion for Sarah to ride and a grey gelding for himself, but after Sarah's unconventional adventure with Mr Hunter, George had given the gelding to Alex.

Alex Hunter had nowhere at the lodge in the woods to stable the gelding, so the horse had remained at Grangeback.

"Can't sleep either, eh Black Guy?" Sarah asked as she hooked the lantern onto a nail beside the stable door. The black Friesian stallion whickered softly at Sarah as she stroked her horse's nose.

"I'm not entirely sure that a dressing gown is designed to be worn in a stable." Alex Hunter's voice made Sarah jump.

She turned round to see him stood at the end of the row of stables.

"What are you doing here?" Sarah frowned at the young hunter.

"Just checking the grounds, I do it every night," Alex shrugged, "Why are you out here?"

"I couldn't sleep," Sarah replied, "How long have you been checking the grounds in the dead of night?"

"A few days," Alex said, trying to sound aloof.

"Since we came back from Chester?" Sarah asked.

"Yes," Alex admitted.

"Mr Hunter -" Sarah began, but Alex held up his hand.

"You can say what you like, but there are people in the house that can and have been hurt because of John Smith. I'm not going to let that happen again if I can help it." Alex said firmly.

"Chivalry will get you killed," Sarah warned as she turned back to Black Guy.

"Maybe, but I would rather die trying to prevent the people in this house from being hurt than lying comfortably in my bed," Mr Hunter said in an off-hand manner.

"It would have been better if I'd never left London," Sarah said, shaking her head.

"No matter where you had been, Forsythe would have done whatever he had to to get his hands on that pocket watch. It could have been much worse. In London, there are all sorts of desperate men who would have quite happily slit your throat for a handful of coins, leaving the lieutenant free to search your baggage," Alex replied as he walked down the row of loose boxes to stand next to Sarah.

"Perhaps," Sarah replied.

"There's no perhaps about it. You might not be able to sleep, but you still need to rest. Come on, I'll walk you back to the house," Mr Hunter said, offering Sarah his arm.

"You think I'll be attacked on my walk back to the house?" Sarah asked in surprise.

"No, I think that if I don't walk you back to the house and lock you in, you'll just double back here when you think I've gone," Alex replied.

Sarah took the offered arm, said goodnight to Black Guy and retrieved the lantern from the nail.

"An invitation came to the house today," Sarah said as they walked.

"Ah, the Tatton Park All Hallows' Eve event?" Alex asked.

"Yes, you got invited as well?" Sarah said.

"No, I'm not part of that social sphere. Nor do I want to be. I'm much happier being left alone to look after the woods, the lake and the Brigadier's estate. I don't need to go around in finery and frippery to know where my value lies or to gain anyone's approval," Alex said tartly.

"You really don't like the upper classes, do you?"

Sarah asked sadly.

"As a group, not particularly. There are individuals I like though. You and the Brigadier, you're not like the others, and there are a few men who I grew up with that are now honourable. They're not too bad," Alex said with a wry smile playing at the corner of his mouth.

"From the way people in Stickleback Hollow speak about you, I didn't realise you had any friends," Sarah said, realising too late how harsh her words were.

"Gruff and illegitimate are crimes that people don't easily forgive you for. The men I know were the boys I went to school with. I wasn't there all that long, but they still sneak away to come and visit. We go hunting or fishing most of the time. I'm sure you'll meet some of them at Tatton Park," Alex said, not taking any offence to what Sarah had said.

By the time they reached the house, Sarah was struggling to keep her eyes open. Talking with Mr Hunter had completely distracted her from thoughts of her parents.

She took the key out of her pocket and unlocked the door.

"Try and get some sleep," Alex said.

"Thank you, and if you see your friends before All

Hallows' Eve, bring them to the house. It would be nice to have some people to talk to at the ball," Sarah yawned.

"All right. Goodnight," Alex said. He waited by the door until Sarah had locked it, relit her candle and extinguished the lantern. He watched her leave the kitchen and the light of the candle moving down the corridor.

He laughed to himself as he walked back to the lodge. When he got back to his home, he didn't go inside. Instead, he went around to the back of the house where there was a hatch to an old cellar was hidden. He had woven leaves and twigs into a fishing net and used it to cover over the hatch.

Unless you knew it was there, you wouldn't be able to distinguish any difference between the fishing net and the woodland floor.

He pulled aside the fishing net and opened the hatch. There was a stone staircase that led down into the old cellar. Mr Hunter often used the cellar to store weapons and food that was being salted or pickled. It was also a good place to hang game birds whilst they matured.

In the far corner of the cellar was a large barrel with a line of salt around the bottom of it. Alex carefully inspected the salt line. When he was happy it hadn't been disturbed, he left the cellar with a jar of pickled beetroot in his hand, then closed the hatch and put the fishing net back in place.

It may have looked strange to anyone watching for a man to retrieve a jar of pickled beetroot in the middle of the night from a hidden cellar, but Mr Hunter reasoned that it would look more suspicious if he had come out of the cellar empty-handed.

Two days after he and Sarah had returned from Chester, George had brought him Colonel Montgomery Baird's pocket watch. The Brigadier had taken it from Sarah's room.

John Smith, or Lady Carol-Ann Margaret de Mandeville, Duchess of Aumale and Montagu as she was better known, was a dangerous woman who desperately wanted to get her hands on that pocket watch.

George knew that as long as Sarah had it, she was in danger. So, he had taken it and given it to Alex to hide, under the strict instruction that he should never tell anyone where it was, no matter what happened to him.

Alex had hidden the pocket watch. But he couldn't shake the feeling that he was being watched. He reasoned that if he were being watched, then so was everyone at

28

Grangeback. So far he hadn't any proof that anyone was watching him or the other people on the estate, but until he got rid of the uneasiness he felt, he was not going to stop patrolling the grounds.

Chapter 3

"What ho, Hunter!" a friendly voice called out to Alex as he sat fishing by the lake. It was mid-afternoon, and the woods had been peaceful until the sound of footsteps tramping through it had broken its serenity.

Mr Hunter turned his head to see Thomas and Edward Egerton walking towards him with Daniel Cooper and Harry Taylor.

"Good morning, what brings you all to Stickleback Hollow?" Alex asked as he set down his rod and went to greet the four men with a handshake each.

"It seemed a pity to spoil such a nice day lounging around at Tatton Park, so we thought we'd come and pay you a visit," Harry grinned.

"Now, why don't I believe that?" Alex said with a raised eyebrow.

Alex had been at school with Harry, Thomas and Daniel. The three hadn't always been friends, but after an incident one night in Chester a few years ago, the country gentlemen had become much warmer in their regard for the huntsman.

Mr Hunter had left school in order to learn about groundskeeping, and he had never really been accepted by the boys he was at school with. He had been visiting Chester when he had seen Mr Taylor and the two Mr Egertons being accosted in the street by two rather unscrupulous characters.

Alex had seen the flash of a blade and intervened. The two men had left with memorable souvenirs on their faces, but they were still alive when they slinked away. Mr Hunter had then delivered the three young men to Tatton Park without saying a word to them.

The next day they had come to visit him at the lodge to apologise for their behaviour up to this point and thank him for saving their lives. Thus their friendship had begun.

It wasn't a friendship that included invitations to social occasions, but they often came to visit the huntsman.

"Well, we heard some rumours that you know the latest edition to the neighbourhood and were curious as to what she's like," Edward shrugged.

"You were curious?" Alex asked, crossing his arms.

"Fine, my mother sent us to question you," Daniel said,

holding up his hands in mock surrender.

"There's not much I can tell you. If you want to know what she's like, go visit the house," Alex replied.

"Don't you think that seems a lot like we're going to call on her?" Thomas frowned.

"Well, that's what you will be doing in essence," Alex half-laughed.

"We're not going to call on her," Daniel said flatly.

"Well, then you'll just have to wait until the ball to meet her," Alex shrugged, "Of course, she'll be very disappointed. She asked if I'd take you up to the house to meet her when you next came to visit."

"You really are a devil sometimes, Hunter," Harry laughed.

"Let me put my rod away, and I'll take you to meet her. She's probably not in the house anyway," Alex said as he turned to pick up his fishing rod.

It didn't take long for the five men to stop at the lodge and for Alex to put away his rod and bait. Mr Hunter led the way from the lodge through the woods around Grangeback. There was a more direct route that they could have taken to reach the house, but Alex walked the four men on a route that he thought would lead them past the places Sarah was most likely to be if she wasn't at the house.

After about twenty minutes of walking, Mr Hunter caught sight of Sarah riding on Black Guy. The pair were racing across the deer park. There had been a few of the older trees felled by high winds, which now made for some interesting obstacles.

Sarah and Black Guy were jumping over the fallen trees. It seemed that Sarah had devised a course that she was taking Black Guy round. The ground had been churned up as Sarah had ridden round the course.

Mr Hunter was torn between berating Sarah for spoiling the lawns that were so carefully maintained and being impressed at how she had turned the lawns into her own cross country course.

"Gentleman, I present the Lady Sarah Montgomery Baird Watson-Wentworth," Alex said with a grin.

The five men stood and watched Sarah riding from a distance for a few minutes. It was clear that she had spent most of her life riding horses and had been properly schooled in the equestrian arts.

Sarah could sense that she was being watched, but she

didn't want to interrupt the rhythm of the round. She waited until she had completed the course before she slowed Black Guy to a walk and looked around.

When she spotted the five men, she turned Black Guy towards them and let the horse have his head as they plodded towards their audience.

"You know Mrs Bosworth will have a fit when she sees that lawn," Alex greeted Sarah when she was close enough that he didn't have to shout.

"No one uses the deer park, not even for walking. Mrs Bosworth won't even know it's not pristine anymore. Unless, of course, you tell her," Sarah replied as she swung herself out of the saddle.

Her face was covered with mud, and her hair was a mess. She was dressed in Moghul breeches and the short boots that the local cobbler had crafted for her, along with one of the shirts and corsets that Miss Baker had made.

She was not what the gentlemen had expected of a titled lady. When Mr Hunter had said that she wouldn't be at the house, they had expected to find her lying on a chaise in the gardens with a book and afternoon tea.

"I won't tell her. Lady Sarah may I present Mr Thomas

Egerton, Mr Edward Egerton, Mr Harry Taylor and Mr Daniel Cooper of Tatton Park," Alex said as he pointed to each of the men in turn.

"Nice to meet you all," Sarah beamed.

"You should probably take Black Guy back to the stables. He looks like he needs a good rub down and a rest," Alex remarked as his four friends stood awkwardly.

"He's worked hard today, come on, I'm sure that Cooky will have prepared tea as well," Sarah said as she started to lead Black Guy back towards Grangeback.

"Was that an invitation to tea?" Edward frowned.

"You expected something a little more formal?" Harry asked in disbelief.

"Well, I mean, most invitations to tea are made to seem like requests," Edward said, shaking his head.

"You'll find that with Lady Sarah, things are always a little different," Mr Hunter said in a low voice before he followed Sarah back towards Grangeback.

Chapter 4

All Hallows' Eve came around a lot faster than Sarah had thought was possible. During the weeks that led up to the ball, the two Egertons had been to visit Sarah a few times. Thomas had brought his wife Charlotte to meet Sarah and Charlotte had introduced her to Mary Pierrepoint – Edward's fiancée.

Mr Taylor didn't live at Tatton Park. He often came to visit his friends, but his family home was in Staffordshire. Mr Cooper lived at Tatton Park with his mother, Ruth, but after word had reached Mrs Cooper about Sarah's apparent wild behaviour, she had forbidden her son from calling on the lady.

Sarah had been kept busy by the constant visits of the Egertons, so time had passed quickly. When she hadn't been taking callers, she had been out on Black Guy taking him over the cross country course.

She hadn't seen very much of Mr Hunter since he had introduced her to his friends. When she had asked the Brigadier about where Mr Hunter was, George had replied,

"I rarely see him at this time of year. He's normally very busy with helping with the harvest."

Two days before the ball, Mrs Bosworth and Cooky had started to fuss over Sarah, talking of her hair, her make-up and what she as going to wear. Sarah had tried to indulge the women, but it had quickly become very tiresome.

By the time All Hallows' Eve arrived, Sarah was dreading the evening. Mrs Bosworth had tried to insist that Sarah start getting ready the moment she awoke. The festivities didn't start until 6 'clock, and Sarah knew it wasn't going to take long for her to prepare herself.

She spent the day out riding, avoiding both Cooky and Mrs Bosworth as much as possible. At 4 o'clock, she returned to the house, covered in sweat and mud, causing Mrs Bosworth to fly into a panic.

Despite the protestations that Sarah would never be ready in time, she was ready to leave the house at 5 o'clock.

She had dressed herself as Mrs Bosworth didn't quite understand how the dress was supposed to be worn.

One of the maids came to pin her hair in place. The fashion was to wear her pinned up in curls, but Sarah thought it was far too fussy. Instead, she had her hair pinned to one

The Mysteries of Stickleback Hollow: All Hallows' Eve in Stickleback Hollow

side and roses were placed between the pins for decoration.

Her face was painted, under a great deal of protest, and she descended the stairs to see the Brigadier was waiting for her.

"You look absolutely divine," he smiled at her and offered his arm to the girl. He led Sarah out to the waiting carriage, and the two set off for Tatton Park.

It was polite to arrive slightly early to the festivities on this occasion. By the time the coach trundled up the drive to the main house, it was a quarter to six.

Most of the guests had already arrived. George held out his hand to help Sarah out of the carriage and led her into the hall.

Tatton Park was much grander than Grangeback. The estate was much bigger as a whole, but Sarah thought that she preferred Grangeback.

The master of ceremonies announced them, and George took Sarah to introduce her to their host.

"Wilbraham, Elizabeth, may I present Lady Sarah. Sarah, this is Wilbraham and Elizabeth Egerton, our hosts for the evening," George said.

"Lady Sarah, how wonderful you were able to attend.

My sons and daughter-in-law have told us so much about you," Elizabeth said as she took Sarah's arm and began to show her off around the room.

Many of the younger women around the room sneered at the dress that Sarah was wearing, though the older women showered her with compliments.

"Lady Sarah, may I introduce you to Lady Szonja, the Countess of Huntingdon. Lady Szonja, this is Lady Sarah Montgomery Baird Watson-Wentworth, she has recently arrived from India," Elizabeth said as they came across a woman that was more finely dressed than any in the room.

"A pleasure, my dear," Lady Szonja said.

"The countess and I are distant cousins on my mother's side," Elizabeth explained.

"You come to visit often, countess?" Sarah asked.

"Life in the south can be so dull and unvaried at times. The north is full of interesting characters though, there always seems to be something going on," Countess Szonja gave her cousin a slight smile.

"Well, that is because all of those who don't fit into London society escape to the north," Elizabeth said lightly.

"It adds such colour to the locality," Szonja smirked.

"What a lovely necklace you have, Countess," Sarah said, changing the subject. She could tell that there was something that the Countess Szonja was alluding to, implying there was a reason that Elizabeth lived in the north instead of the south.

"Why thank you, my dear, it was a gift from a young prince from Hungary. He was such a dear man. He was too far down the line of succession to ever be a real prospect to be king, but he was a darling creature. He died earlier this year, it was such a tragedy," the countess said sadly.

"I'm so sorry," Sarah wasn't sure what else to say.

"Thank you, my dear. He used to write me such wonderful letters. You heard about the Danube flooding the city of Pest early this year? He was in the city at the time, he drowned trying to help others escape," the countess looked close to tears as she spoke.

"He was an example to us all," Elizabeth said gently as she patted her cousin's hand.

"Yes, he was. I'm sorry; if you will both excuse me for a moment," Szonja said as she rushed from the room.

"I'm sorry; I didn't mean to upset her," Sarah felt awful for causing the countess such distress.

"My dear lady, you did nothing wrong. You couldn't have known. Szonja was engaged to the prince at one point, but her mother didn't approve of the match, he wasn't prominent enough for her. So she was married to the Count of Huntingdon. He was much older than she was, of course, but she never gave up her relationship with the prince. It was thought that once the count died, the two would be able to reunite. The count passed away last October. Szonja made plans to travel to Hungary in May to meet with the prince and discuss announcing their betrothal, but he died in March. It all seems so cruel. If you will excuse me, my lady, I must make sure she is all right," Elizabeth said. She curtsied to Sarah and then followed the path her cousin had taken through the ballroom.

Sarah had never felt more awkward in her life as she stood looking helplessly around the room. People were staring at her as they milled around, and more than a few of them were whispering behind their hands as they stared.

"My dear Sarah, what a delight to see you in such finery," Doctor Hales called out as he pushed his way through the crowded room to greet Sarah.

"Doctor, how good to see you," Sarah said with relief.

41

"I don't think you know my sons, may I introduce you to Richard and Gordon. They're wretched lazy, but they're not a bad sort," the doctor said as he beckoned for his two sons to come forward.

"We've heard a lot about you, my lady," Richard said as he bowed to Sarah.

"I haven't seen either of you in Stickleback Hollow before," Sarah said as Richard and Gordon finished bowing to her.

"They're both studying at University. Richard is studying at Oxford and Gordon at Cambridge. As you can imagine, things get very tense around the time of the Boat Race," the doctor winked at Sarah.

"I'm sorry; I don't know anything about the Boat Race," Sarah said apologetically.

"Ah, of course, you're unlikely to be talking about the events between the universities in the depths of the Indian jungle," the doctor said as he rubbed his forehead, "It's really a lot of harmless fun between the two universities. It was started by a chap called Charles Merivale who challenged one of his fellow Harrow alumni, Charles Wordsworth to a boat race. Merivale was at St John's, Cambridge and Wordsworth was at

42

Christ Church, Oxford."

"The first race was at Henley-on-Thames, which really was an ideal location for the race to take place," Gordon explained.

"Don't be ridiculous, Westminster to Putney is where the second race was held because we beat you so thoroughly in the first. It proved to be a much better location," Richard argued. The two boys began a rather heated argument about the race, which, to Sarah's surprise, drew in many of the men from around the room.

There was soon such a noise caused by the guests over the subject of the Boat Race that Sarah had to remove herself from the ballroom.

"It's rather surprising what people in high society will choose to argue about." a familiar voice said as Sarah sat down in a chair and tried to gather her thoughts.

"Mr Cooper, how nice to see you," Sarah said pleasantly. Sarah had stepped out of the ballroom into the corridor where Daniel Cooper was stood looking at some of the portraits.

"The subject of the Boat Race is something that I am sure will cause more arguments as it continues. It seems one of

43

those things destined to become tradition," Daniel sighed and shook his head.

"You aren't tempted to join the discussion?" Sarah asked.

"No, I am much happier staying away from the ballroom, my mother is determined to introduce me to all the young women that she can. It is safer out here in the hall," Daniel said dryly.

"If she can't find you in the ballroom, surely this is the first place she would look," Sarah frowned.

"Ah, you overestimate my mother. Whilst there are so many people to socialise with of such high pedigree, my mother will not be actively looking for me. The moment she spots me, she will endeavour to push as many young ladies into my company as possible," Daniel sighed.

"I would have thought that would be the dream of every young man," Sarah gave Daniel a wry smile.

"Beauty and breeding are not everything. There seems to be a rather severe drought of intelligence amongst the current eligible young ladies," Daniel said, shaking his head.

"I see, and Mr Daniel Cooper is in need of a companion with intelligence?" Sarah smiled.

44

"I do not wish to be saddled with another woman like my mother," Daniel sighed.

"And she does not want you to connect with a wild women either," Sarah smirked.

"Thomas and Edward told you about that then?" Daniel said with a grimace.

"They weren't very good at lying about where you were. After their third visit, they told me the truth," Sarah smiled.

"You aren't insulted?" Daniel asked with surprise.

"Not particularly. I was surprised at how much control mothers seem to have over their sons here, but if someone wishes to form an opinion on my character based on gossip and hearsay, I have no intention of attempting to change their mind," Sarah shrugged.

"You really aren't like any other woman I've ever met," Daniel said in slight awe of Sarah, "Would you do the honour of accompanying me to dinner?"

Chapter 5

The sound of the dinner gong was lost in the noise of the Boat Race argument in the ballroom. Those who were exploring other rooms, out on the patio and in the corridors heard the sound of the gong.

Sarah took Daniel's arm and accompanied him to the dining room. Countess Szonja, Elizabeth Egerton and a handful of other people were already in the dining room as Sarah and Daniel took their seats.

After fifteen minutes of waiting at the table, Elizabeth left the dining room to find out where the rest of her guests were. A few minutes after she left the room, a rather muted party of men entered followed by a group of unimpressed women.

"Elizabeth will have quietly told the ladies that the gentlemen had delayed dinner by fifteen minutes – an unforgivable faux pas when arguing over something so trivial," Daniel whispered to Sarah as the lady cast her eyes over the men and women as they sat down.

46

"Lady Sarah, wonderful to see you!" Mr Harry Taylor said as he sat down on the other side of Sarah, "May I introduce you to my fiancée, Miss Elizabeth Wessex."

"A pleasure to meet you, Lady Sarah," Elizabeth Wessex smiled at Sarah as she sat down next to Harry.

"Ah Lady Sarah, we saw the Brigadier but didn't know where you had got to," Thomas Egerton beamed as he sat down opposite Sarah with his wife, Charlotte. Edward and his fiancée, Mary, sat down on the other side of Daniel.

"Lady Sarah, may we introduce you to our brother, Captain Wilbraham Egerton, who is currently serving Her Majesty in the army," Edward said as he presented a tall, bearded man with slightly weather-beaten skin.

"Lady Sarah, my brothers tell me you were in India with your father. I'm sorry to hear that a man like Colonel Montgomery Baird has passed." Wilbraham said as he sat down beside Thomas.

"Thank you," Sarah said, trying to avoid talking about her parents.

"How are you finding England?" Charlotte asked.

"It's rather different to what I expected," Sarah said delicately.

47

"Quite a culture shock, I expect, though you have certainly caused a sensation this evening with your beautiful gown," Mary said with a warm smile.

"It really is quite stunning," Charlotte agreed.

"I hear that you met our cousin Szonja, she seems to be very taken with you," Wilbraham said.

"Making a favourable impression on the countess? Now that is an achievement," Harry said in astonishment.

Sarah felt a little lost in the sea of conversation as it developed. She focused on listening and eating. Harry, Daniel, Wilbraham, Edward and Thomas seemed content to steer the direction of the conversation with input from Mary, Charlotte and Elizabeth, but none of them demanded too much from Sarah in the way of response.

"My grandmother has been sending me clippings from the Spectator over the last few months," Mary said during a lull in the conversation.

"Oh, the latest offering from Mr Dickens, what's it called?" Charlotte asked intensely

"Nicholas Nickleby. The countess brought the past copies of the Spectator with her so that we could read them. I preferred his work in The Pickwick Papers personally,"

48

Wilbraham said between mouthfuls.

"Of course, it's a work of fiction; it takes realties and over dramatises them for effect," Edward said dismissively.

"Though that is true of other writers, I don't think that is the case with Mr Dickens. There was a scandal at Bowes Academy in Yorkshire that my friends were telling me about when Mr Dickens story was first published," Harry countered.

"A scandal?" Sarah asked.

"Bowes Academy was prosecuted and investigated for neglect after two of their pupils went blind," Harry explained.

"And what does that have to do with Mr Dickens?" Charlotte asked.

"Well he went to visit the school, and after visiting it, he began writing. I'm inclined to believe that it is far more realistic than we would like to think," Harry said seriously.

"Well, you can't expect all schools to be the equal of Eaton and Harrow," Mary said lightly.

"But of course, the terrible conditions in Yorkshire boarding schools are not the only theme in the pieces I've read," Daniel replied.

"Ah, you're referring to the question about what defines a gentleman!" Thomas said, slamming his hand down

49

on the edge of the table.

"Well, considering our current situation, it does pose an excellent question, wouldn't you admit?" Daniel smiled,

"You're referring to me?" Sarah asked.

"Well, at least to the way in which your reputation is regarded by some of our present company," Daniel shrugged.

"I would have thought you were talking about Mr Hunter," Elizabeth said as she drank from her wine glass.

"Why would it apply to Mr Hunter?" Mary frowned, "Surely no one could mistake him for a gentleman."

Before any of the company could reply, the master of ceremonies banged his gavel on the edge of the table. Silence descended over the room as Wilbraham Egerton senior rose to his feet.

"My dear friends, it is wonderful to see you gathered again on this All Hallows' Eve. We have all eaten, and now it is our turn to go out and feed those who have less than we do."

A murmur of approval ran around the room.

"If you would all be so kind as to don your cloaks and hats and meet us in the hall. Then we shall walk down to the village," Wilbraham said and sat down again.

"To the hallway then," Daniel said.

Chapter 6

It took a surprisingly long time for most of the invited guests to leave the dinner table. Daniel, Sarah, Wilbraham, Thomas, Edward, Harry, Elizabeth, Charlotte and Mary were the first to leave the dining room.

The footmen brought the women their cloaks, their fur muffs and their bonnets, and the hats and the cloaks that belonged to the men. When they were all wrapped up, they stepped outside to wait for the rest of the party.

There was frost in the air that told of approaching snow. Sarah shivered even more than normal as they stood outside, waiting for the rest of the party to assemble. The silk dress was much more comfortable to wear than the other formal dresses that Sarah owned, but it was not as warm.

The layers of petticoats and material made the dresses a lot warmer than the Indian style silk creation that Sarah wore. She had the long fur riding cape wrapped around her shoulders to try and keep out the worst of the cold.

After ten minutes of waiting, Sarah was shivering

badly. Daniel removed his own cloak and draped it over Sarah's without saying a word.

It took half an hour before all of the guests of the Egerton's had assembled outside. When everyone was there, Wilbraham and Elizabeth Egerton led the way down the drive.

A cart was driven behind the large number of guests as they walked. It was stacked with food and drink. Some of it had been provided by the house, and the rest had been provided by the Egertons' guests.

Once they were moving, Sarah felt much warmer and gave Daniel back his cloak. The Brigadier was walking with the doctor and his sons not far behind Mr and Mrs Egerton. Sarah and the others were towards the back near the cart. Wilbraham was escorting the countess and had disappeared into the throng of people.

As they walked, Sarah noticed that there seemed to be far more men than women in the party.

"It's a rather mixed blessing. Every gentleman wants a son to carry on his family name, but nearly every family in the area has far more sons than daughters. There isn't just a drought of intelligent women here; there is a general drought of any women here," Daniel explained.

"Our sister, Charlotte, has had many suitors coming to call on her in the last few months," Edward said.

"So many that mother and father had her sent to London to keep her from behind pestered for a while. Her friend, Margaret Cust, went with her. Then our youngest brother, Charles, followed Margaret to London," Thomas laughed.

"He didn't tell anyone that he was going; he just disappeared one day and reappeared in London," Mary giggled.

"Charles always was a bit of a hopeless romantic," Harry said, shaking his head.

"Mrs Cooper was very disappointed when Charlotte went to town; she's had great plans of marrying Daniel and Charlotte off to one another ever since she came to live here," Elizabeth chuckled. Daniel blushed, and Sarah felt an odd sinking sensation in her stomach at the idea of Daniel marrying someone else.

"I'm surprised she hasn't had a fit already, what with the two of you walking together," Charlotte observed.

"Mother's far too busy trying to ingratiate herself with Mr and Mrs Mullaney to pay any attention to me this evening," Daniel said in a bitter tone.

"Mr and Mrs Mullaney?" Sarah frowned.

"Abigail and Johnathen. They are very well connected at court," Daniel replied dryly.

"Maybe we should spend some time trying to find a suitable suitor for your mother in London society. At least then you wouldn't have to have her flittering around you all the time," Thomas grinned.

"There are men that would be interested in a woman as silly as she is?" Daniel frowned.

"We can speak to the countess; she seems to know everyone and everything when it comes to matrimonial matters," Charlotte said eagerly.

"Maybe we should send her off to New York on the SS Great Western. She could meet someone of the journey over or find some gaudy member of the nouveau riche American social scene to sweep her off her feet," Elizabeth giggled more.

"Maybe we should talk about something more interesting than getting rid of my mother," Daniel sighed, shaking his head.

"How much further is it?" Sarah asked, changing the subject.

"That's strange; we should have reached the village by now. It's not that far from the house really. In fact, Tatton Village is in the other direction," Thomas frowned as he looked around wildly.

"Bertie, where are we going?" Edward called out to the cart driver.

"The master told us we'd be heading to Stickleback Hollow rather than Tatton Village this year. Said there was something of a surprise being organised for us there," Bertie replied.

"We're walking all the way to Stickleback Hollow?" Elizabeth gasped.

"We're more than halfway there if that's the case," Sarah said.

"Well, that's something, though my shoes will be ruined before we get back to Tatton Park." Mary sighed.

After walking for almost an hour, the twinkling lights of Stickleback Hollow could be seen through the trees.

Music filled the air as the party grew closer to the village, and the Reverend Percy Butterfield was waiting to greet the party.

"Tonight we celebrate All Hallows' Eve with a festival

56

of dancing and delights. We shall break bread together, remember the souls of all those who have passed and give to those who are less fortunate than ourselves," the reverend declared as the cart of food trundled into the square.

Miss Baker and her sons were there, as were Wilson and Emma from the inn. Mrs Bosworth and Cooky had come down to the village from Grangeback, and even Constable Evans was in attendance.

"Where is Hunter, I wonder," Thomas said as he scanned the assembled village for his friend.

"You know he can't stand parties. He's probably holed up in his lodge, safe from all the frivolity," Harry said, clapping his hands.

"Lady Sarah, my dear, come meet these lovely young gentlemen," Countess Szonja called out to Sarah, beckoning to her from the other side of the square.

Sarah gave Daniel a weak smile and excused herself to join the countess.

"My dear, this is Mr Stuart Moore, Mr Gregory Kitts, Mr Samuel Jones and Mr Jake Walker. They're all sons belonging to one house or another in the neighbourhood," the countess smiled.

57

"A pleasure to meet you," Sarah said. She tried to sound as genuine as she could, but she couldn't help but glance over to where Daniel was stood. The young man didn't look happy as he watched the four men talking to Sarah, but there was nothing he could do about it.

"Cheer up, as soon as the dancing starts, you can steal her away," Harry hissed in Daniel's ear.

"Watch out, here comes your mother," Thomas whispered.

"Daniel Cooper! There you are. Where have you been hiding? No never mind that now. Come with me, Mr Mullaney wants to introduce you to his niece. She's visiting from Essex of all places," Mrs Ruth Cooper could talk at great length without need of a response. She frequently held conversations that lasted for hours during which only her voice participated. Daniel was used to it and simply sighed as his mother seized him by the wrist and dragged him off to introduce him to whatever woman she had decided he was destined to marry this week.

Sarah watched as Daniel was dragged away by his mother and felt her heart sink. She glanced over at the countess and couldn't help but crease her brow.

"Countess, what happened to your necklace?" Sarah asked.

"Oh, I took that off before we left Tatton Park. It's far too valuable to wear whilst walking across half of Cheshire. My maid is sat guarding it now," the countess said with a wave of her hand.

"Excuse me countess, gentlemen, but I need to borrow the Lady Sarah for a moment if I may," Constable Evans said politely as he approached the group.

"Is everything all right, constable?" the countess asked in alarm.

"Everything is quite all right, I merely need to speak to her ladyship about something that happened earlier today," the constable smiled reassuringly at the countess.

Sarah followed the constable away from the festivities to the police house. When they were inside, Constable Evans shut the door and sighed heavily.

"What is it, Arwyn?" Sarah frowned.

"Have you seen Mr Hunter today?" he asked worriedly.

"Alex? No, I haven't seen him for a few days. Why? What's going on?" Sarah felt panic rising in her chest.

"No one has seen him for several days. I went to the lodge this morning, and the whole place is deserted. His horse isn't at Grangeback either," Arwyn said gravely.

"Have you asked the Brigadier? Surely if Mr Hunter was going somewhere, he would tell George first," Sarah said, trying to dismiss the fears that were swirling in her brain.

"No, I haven't mentioned it to the Brigadier yet. It could all be perfectly innocent, he may just have gone down to London on personal business, or be spending a few days in Chester," the constable said with a shrug.

"But something tells you that it isn't perfectly innocent," Sarah said flatly.

"I can't put my finger on what it is, but there is something not quite right here. It's not just Mr Hunter disappearing. There are other things as well that are very suspicious," the constable said, scratching his head.

"Like what?" Sarah asked.

"People have reported seeing strange things in the mist. Hearing things going bump in the night, dogs barking at nothing, things moving on their own. I know they say that the veil between the living and the dead is at its thinnest this time of year, but I never believed in that until now," Arwyn said nervously.

"You think that there is something to the old superstitions?" Sarah asked

"Maybe, maybe not, but I don't like what's going on one bit – work of evil forces or not," Constable Evans said firmly.

"Well, we can hardly go around arresting goblins and ghouls," Sarah teased.

"You'll be going around arresting no one. I'm still in trouble with the Chief Constable over your missing jewellery," Arwyn said in a warning tone. Before Sarah could reply, a horrific scream cut through the air.

Sarah and Constable Evans looked at each other with dread before dashing out of the police house and rushing in the direction of the scream.

Chapter 7

The screaming had stopped by the time Constable Evans and Lady Sarah got outside.

"Where did it come from?" Sarah asked, looking around the dark streets of Stickleback Hollow for any sign.

"Oh, Constable Evans! There you are!" Miss Baker gasped. She was out of breath and clearly had been running to find help.

"Miss Baker, was that you screaming?" Sarah asked with concern.

"No, it was coming from the forest," Miss Baker gasped.

"You go back to the square and keep everyone there; I'll go investigate the woods," Constable Evans said calmly to the two ladies.

"I'm not letting you go alone," Sarah snorted.

"My lady, it could be – oh, very well," Arwyn sighed. The constable knew better than to try and argue with the stubborn lady of Grangeback.

"Be careful, my lady, constable," Miss Baker called after Constable Evans and Lady Sarah as the two rushed off towards the forest. Sarah was glad that she wasn't wearing the dresses with petticoats now, though the modified sari was not very easy to run in.

Miss Baker watched the pair with great concern before she returned to the square to try and keep the people of Stickleback Hollow calm and tell the Brigadier what was going on.

As Arwyn and Sarah drew closer to the woods, the two slowed down. It was dark, and there was only so much light that was cast by the lantern that Arwyn carried,

"The screaming can't have come from very far in; the sound wouldn't have carried to the police house if it was too deep in the trees," Arwyn reasoned as they moved slowly through the trees.

"Look, there are footprints here that look like they belong to a woman," Sarah said, pointing at some deep impressions in the mud. They quickly disappeared amongst the darkness and the undergrowth.

"I can't see where they go. I wish Mr Hunter was here. He could follow footsteps over water," Constable Evans sighed.

"Well, we'll have to make do without him for now. I can't see signs of anything else being in the woods. Are there any tunnels, caves, mine shafts or drops that she could have fallen into or over the Edge of?" Sarah asked.

"No, not down here. It's mostly flat in this part of the wood, but it stretches all the way to the Edge that goes up behind the village," Arwyn said as he looked in the direction of Stickleback Edge.

"There are drop-offs and other dangers up there?" Sarah asked. She hadn't been anywhere near the Edge since moving to Stickleback Hollow.

"There's an old mine up there, drop-offs, caves, and if you believe the local legend, there are knights sleeping under it," the constable said dryly, "A woman's scream wouldn't have carried down here from the Edge though."

"So whoever was screaming has disappeared," Sarah sighed.

"Let's go back to the square and see if anyone is missing or has seen anyone come out of the wood," the constable said and led the way back to the village.

Sarah lingered for a moment in the woods. The hair on

the back of her neck were stood up on end, she felt like she was being watched. Sarah used to get the same feeling when she was in the forests of India and the big cats that called the trees their home were watching her.

She couldn't see anything, but still couldn't shake the feeling she was being watched. She shivered and pulled her cloak more tightly around her, then followed the Constable back to Stickleback Hollow.

"Lady Sarah!" Charlotte called out as Sarah stepped out of the treeline with the constable.

"What is it, Charlotte?" Sarah asked as the wife of Thomas almost collapsed into the lady's arms.

"Mr Cooper and Mr Taylor are both missing," Charlotte gasped.

"Missing?" Sarah frowned.

"Yes, they were both talking to Mrs Cooper, and now they are nowhere to be seen," Charlotte said desperately.

"Don't worry yourself, Mrs Egerton; they probably went into the woods to investigate the scream. If you can tell me where they were talking to Mrs Cooper, I can go after them and bring them safely out again," Constable Evans said in a comforting voice.

"Oh thank you, constable, they were over here," Charlotte said with relief and led Arwyn across the square to where Harry and Daniel had last been seen.

Sarah stood in the square and bit her lip. Something was very wrong, the celebratory atmosphere had disappeared, and instead, there was now a feeling of fear in the air.

Chapter 8

Constable Evans searched the woods for half an hour before giving up and returning to the square. He couldn't see any sign of Mr Taylor or Mr Cooper amongst the trees.

Arwyn wasn't too worried as he walked back to the village. He hadn't seen anything suspicious amongst the trees and imagined that if the two gentlemen had ventured into the trees, then they would have returned to the party in the square by now.

He kicked through the leaves as he walked. Most of the trees had lost their leaves, and the ground was covered in moist red and brown leaves. There were patches of mud that appeared between the leaves, but there was no sign that anyone had walked into the woods, except for the constable.

When Constable Evans stepped out of the trees, he could tell from the looks on the faces around him that the two gentlemen hadn't returned. The chief constable, Captain Thomas Jonnes Smith, was keeping Mrs Cooper and Miss Wessex calm.

The sight of Constable Evans walking out of the forest alone sent the two women into fits of hysterics. Charlotte and Mary gently coaxed Mrs Cooper and Miss Wessex away from staring eyes as the chief constable walked up to Arwyn.

"Well?" he demanded in a regimental tone.

"There's no sign of anyone in the woods. There was no woman who screamed, and there is no evidence that the two gentlemen are in there either," the constable said.

He was always nervous when the chief constable was around, but with an unknown woman screaming in the forest and two gentlemen vanishing shortly after, he was much more nervous than he normally was.

"Are you skilled at tracking people in dark woods?" Captain Jonnes Smith asked

"No, sir," Constable Evans said with a sigh.

"Then we need someone who is. Where's that hunter that you arrested before?" the chief constable asked gruffly.

"He's not in town, sir. No one has seen him for days," Arwyn replied.

"Then we organise these men to search the woods for the screaming woman and the missing gentleman. The ladies will have to be taken somewhere safe whilst we conduct the search," Captain Jonnes Smith instructed.

"They can go to Grangeback. They will be safe enough there," Sarah volunteered as she interrupted the conversation between the policemen.

"Lady Montgomery Baird Watson-Wentworth, you are included in the women that will be going to Grangeback. Your reckless actions that led to the arrest of Constable Cartwright were questionable for a lady in your position. Parading around the woods at night with a group of men searching for three missing people is completely out of the question," the chief constable said sternly.

"Chief Constable, there is nothing improper about searching for missing people," Sarah argued.

"Mr Walker, Mr Moore, if you would be kind enough to escort all the ladies to the house of Grangeback and ensure that they remain there," Captain Jonnes Smith glared at Sarah as he spoke.

Mr Jake Walker took Lady Sarah's arm and led her away from the chief constable. There was no point in Sarah resisting her escort. The other ladies were frightened, and there was nothing to be gained from causing a fuss and disturbing them more than they already were.

Sarah could hear the chief constable gathering the men together and dividing them into search parties as she was led away.

The walk to Grangeback felt like it took forever to Sarah. The two gentlemen that were escorting the ladies didn't know where they were going in the dark, so it was down to Bosworth and Mrs Bosworth to lead the way with Cook.

Bosworth was excused from searching the forest because of his head injury, but the rest of the male household staff from Grangeback had stayed behind in the village to help search the woods.

The women and children from the village walked with the ladies from the ball to Grangeback. If something or someone was lurking in the woods, then it wasn't safe for women or children to be left alone in their houses whilst the men scoured the woods.

They were forced to take the long road up to the house instead of the country tracks that Sarah would normally have used. By the time they reached the house, the children were moaning about their feet and the cold.

The moment Sarah stepped through the door into the house; Mr Walker relinquished her arm and went to check that

70

the other entrances to the house were secure.

Mr Moore stood by the door and made sure that all of the women and children had safely arrived, then he shut and bolted the front door.

There were so many women in distress and so much noise and confusion that it was easy for Sarah to slip away from the congregation. She walked up the stairs to her rooms and locked the door behind her.

She pulled off the sari she wore, took out the pins in her hair and slipped her feet out of the shoes she wore. She carefully draped the sari over the back of one of the chairs in the room. She had left her long cloak downstairs in the hall, but her shorter cape was in her room.

She changed into her riding clothes and slipped the short cape about her shoulders. When she was dressed, she opened one of the windows and climbed out of it.

The masonry provided ample hand and footholds as Sarah climbed slowly down to the ground. She kept low as she skirted around the edge of the house and then turned down towards the stable.

The chief constable had made it quite clear that Sarah searching the woods for the missing gentlemen as a member of one of the search parties was out of the question, but no one had mentioned Sarah riding through the woods on her own.

She saddled Black Guy quickly and set off at a trot towards the forest. She took one of the lanterns from the stable to light her way and she had her pistol, with spare powder and shot, in the purse that was tied around her waist.

Sarah didn't know where Daniel and Harry were, but something told her she should start looking in the most unlikely place. She turned Black Guy towards the northern tip of the estate and rode towards Swallow's End.

Chapter 9

Nobody saw Sarah sneak down to the stable, and nobody saw the lady riding her black steed through the darkness. She didn't rush. The sound of Black Guy galloping might have brought men from the house to stop her, so instead she let Black Guy pick his way through the darkness at a walk.

The night was still clear, she could see the stars and the moon overhead, and the air was crisp and cool. The trees cast shadows that danced in the patches of moonlight and the glow that the lantern cast. It was an eerie experience. The disappearances had changed the atmosphere around the grounds. Sarah felt nervous as she rode. The slightest sound made her heart race and Black Guy skittered at shadows.

She was approaching the lawn where her cross country course was set when she saw something large moving about. She pulled hard on Black Guy's reins and sat perfectly still as she watched the shape move.

It was big but fast. Then she heard it snort and her

73

heart started again. It was a horse. She nudged Black Guy forward with her calves and slowly the pair approached the horse.

As she got closer and the light of the lantern was cast over the horse, Sarah saw it was Harald, Alex Hunter's horse.

"Harald, what are you doing out here?" Sarah asked, more to calm herself than anything else. She stopped and dismounted from Black Guy. She threw his reins over his head and led him towards Harald, holding up the lantern. The grey gelding was covered with foam and sweat. He had clearly been terrified by something. There was no sign of Alex near the horse or the cross country course.

"Mr Hunter!" Sarah called out as she took Harald's reins in the same hand as Black Guy's. There was no reply. Sarah walked around in circles trying to pick up the trail of hoof prints that Harald had left.

The horse had spent a lot of time wandering backwards and forwards across the lawn, after about ten minutes of following the trail, she found the path that Harald had taken from the forest.

She slowly led both horses as she followed Harald's tracks. They led up the lawn to Swallow's End. The horses twitched nervously as Sarah neared the trees. Rather than trying to lead both the horses into the woods, Sarah tied them both to the closest tree and continued on her own.

With the horses securely tied to the tree, she could draw her pistol out of the purse that hung from her waist. She walked with the lantern in one hand and the pistol in the other.

Sarah was shaking slightly as she followed the hoof prints. The ground was soft and the speed Harald had moved at had left clear signs of where he had passed, even with the blanket of leaves on the ground.

She kept one eye on the ground and the other on where she was going. As she got closer to the End, the hoof prints had paw prints beside them. Sarah couldn't tell whether they were the paw prints of dogs or wolves just by looking at them.

She gripped the pistol tighter as she followed the trail. She pricked up her ears to listen for the slightest sound. It now made sense that Harald had fled and left Alex behind.

Sarah didn't dare call out, but as she got through the trees, she found she didn't need to. She found the body of Alex Hunter lying on the ground, bleeding profusely from the shoulder.

There were teeth and claw marks on his shoulder, sweat was covering his forehead, and he was breathing heavily.

"Mr Hunter!" Sarah hissed sadly as she knelt down beside him and tried to examine the wound.

"Lady Sarah?" Alex asked. He sounded delirious as he spoke.

"I'm here, come on, I'll take you back to Grangeback," Sarah said gently. She put her pistol back into her purse and struggled to get Alex to his feet.

The big man staggered as he was finally heaved to his feet. Sarah took his good arm and put it around her neck as she helped him walk back to where the horses were.

Alex wasn't in a fit state to ride, but with great effort, Sarah managed to get him to lie over Harald's back and then led the horses back to Grangeback.

As she reached the front steps of the house, the doors were flung open, and Mr Walker and Mr Moore came out with dark expressions on their faces.

As they helped Mr Hunter into the house, the sound of voices behind her, told Sarah that the men had returned from their search.

There was no jubilation in the voices as they approached, which told Sarah that they hadn't found Mr Cooper or Mr Taylor in the trees.

Arwyn came over to Sarah to ask about where Alex had been. She told him about the tracks and signs at Swallows' End. Arwyn was in two minds about whether he should chide Sarah for leaving the house, but he knew that it wouldn't stop her or change what had happened.

Mrs Cooper was in the drawing room and burst into a crying fit when news was brought that no sign of Daniel was found. Miss Wessex had been taken upstairs to rest, so Charlotte Egerton went upstairs to tell her that Harry hadn't been found.

When Alex was put to bed in one of the spare rooms, Sarah went down to the drawing room and was met with the screeching face of Ruth Cooper coming towards her.

"It's your fault, you terrible creature! You've done something with him! Bring him back!" Ruth cried and tried to pull at Sarah's hair and clothes, but Sarah stepped back from her as the young men came forward to restrain the hysterical woman.

"When Mr Cooper and Mr Taylor went missing, Lady

Sarah was with me, Mrs Cooper. Their disappearance has nothing to do with her," Constable Evans said gently.

"Harlot! Where is my son? Bring him back!" Ruth screamed

"Mrs Bosworth, please take Mrs Cooper upstairs to rest." the Brigadier said in a big voice that sounded over the sound of the weeping mother.

"Yes, brigadier." Mrs Bosworth said and with the help of Mr Walker and Mr Moore, took Mrs Cooper out of the room.

Chapter 10

Sarah didn't feel very comfortable sitting in the drawing room whilst the ladies and gentlemen discussed what was to be done to find Mr Cooper and Mr Taylor.

Captain Jonnes Smith had made sure that he took Constable Evans and the Brigadier out of the room to talk to them both and Bosworth had been given strict instructions that Sarah was not to be allowed to follow them.

Though Lady Sarah was curious about what was being said, she had something more pressing to take care of. She made her way up the stairs to the rooms where Mr Hunter was resting.

"So, what do you think of Mrs Cooper?" Alex asked as Sarah opened the door.

"How did you know it was me?" Sarah frowned.

"The sound of your footsteps. Everybody walks differently, you can tell who is coming be listening to the sound of their steps," Alex grinned.

"Mrs Cooper is – interesting," Sarah said slowly as she

79

sat down beside Mr Hunter's bed.

"You don't have to be polite about her. She certainly holds no regard for you, so why bother showing restraint in return?" Alex asked.

"It doesn't matter how rude someone else is, it doesn't mean I have to follow their example," Sarah shrugged.

"You're a better person than I," Alex replied, shaking his head.

"How do you know she doesn't like me?" Sarah frowned.

"I heard her screaming a moment ago," Alex said dryly.

"Oh, I see," Sarah pursed her lips and looked slightly uncomfortable.

"I wouldn't worry too much about her though, after all, you're a titled lady with a great fortune. Mrs Cooper can hardly do anything to damage your good standing," Mr Hunter said with a gleam in his eye.

"True, I can quite happily destroy my good standing myself," Sarah grinned.

"You didn't need to come and see me, you know," Alex said as Sarah relaxed.

"I thought you were dead when I first saw you up by

Swallow's End, I just wanted to make sure that you were all right," Sarah shrugged.

"People will talk, it's not proper for young ladies to take care of injured hunters. You have maids and a doctor to do that," Alex said gruffly.

"I was raised to make sure that friends are okay after they were hurt, regardless of where they came from," Sarah said firmly.

"You really had an interesting upbringing out in India," Mr Hunter said, shaking his head.

"Why were you up at Swallow's End?" Sarah asked.

"No reason in particular," Alex tried to shrug, but the pain of his injuries turned the shrug into a wince.

"Did you see what attacked you?" Sarah didn't press him for a more convincing answer.

"Three dogs, at least they looked like dogs. They were big and came out of the night with almost no warning," Mr Hunter shifted in the bed and tried to sit up. He tried to move twice, but ended up falling back down on the pillows in pain.

"Stop trying to move. Your injuries are barely closed. If you keep moving you'll just end up bleeding again," Sarah scolded him.

"Why was Mrs Cooper shouting so much before?" Alex asked as he resigned himself to lying in bed.

"Mr Cooper and Mr Taylor are missing. They vanished from the All Hallows' Eve celebrations in the square," Sarah explained.

"I see," Alex frowned and started to try and move again.

"What are you doing?" Sarah said crossly.

"Someone needs to go find them both," Mr Hunter said as he struggled to lie on his side.

"The men have been out looking for them both. They've found nothing. They sent the ladies back to the house," Sarah said crossly as she tried to push Alex back in the bed.

"Then how did you find me?" Alex asked as he grabbed hold of Sarah's wrist. She was surprised by how strong his grip was, even in his weakened condition.

"I snuck out of the house to look for them," Sarah said with a frown.

"Harry and Daniel go missing and can't be found, so you go out on your own to look for them?" Mr Hunter asked in annoyance.

"If I hadn't, you would still be lying in the forest bleeding," Sarah said flatly as she pulled her wrist free of Mr Hunter's grasp.

"How long have they been missing?" Alex asked.

"A few hours now. Constable Evans and I couldn't find any sign of them in the forest. There was a woman who screamed in the trees too, close to the village, but there is no sign of her either," Sarah sighed.

"And three dangerous dogs running around in the darkness as well. I can't stay in bed, Sarah," Alex said. He struggled to get up one last time, and fresh blood seeped through the bandages that were wrapped around his shoulder and back.

"Mr Hunter, what do you think you are doing?" the doctor roared as he came into the room.

"I'm going to look for Mr Taylor and Mr Cooper," Mr Hunter said as he managed to sit on the edge of the bed.

"You are doing no such thing. You are staying in bed and resting. If you won't do it voluntarily, then I will have you tied to the bed," the doctor said sternly.

Sarah quietly stood and left the room as the doctor, and Mr Hunter argued about him remaining in bed. Sarah thought about returning to her rooms, but she felt it was unfair on the Brigadier to leave him with a house full of distraught women and dissenting men of importance.

Sarah sighed to herself and slowly walked back down to the drawing room. Nothing had changed since she had left. Miss Wessex was still sat with Charlotte and Mary; the men were stood in groups talking with frowns on their faces.

"Ah, Lady Sarah, there you are," Countess Szonja said as Sarah entered the room.

"Countess," Sarah said in reply.

"I've never been to Grangeback before, take me on a tour of the house," the countess said firmly as she took Sarah by the arm and escorted her from the room.

Chapter 11

Sarah led Countess Szonja around the house and showed her all the rooms. Mrs Bosworth had taken Sarah on a tour of the old manor house when she had first moved in, and the young lady had retained all of the information that Mrs Bosworth had imparted.

Sarah told the countess the history of each of the rooms as they passed through them, and gave detailed histories of each of the portraits.

"Where is your portrait?" the countess asked as they reached the end of the gallery where the brigadier's portrait hung beside Lucy and Helen Webb-Kneelingroach.

"I don't have one," Sarah shrugged.

"Well, that needs changing," Szonja said firmly.

By the time that the tour was finished, Constable Evans, Brigadier Webb-Kneelingroach and Chief Constable Captain Jonnes Smith had returned to the drawing room.

"Ah, countess, we were just discussing what should be done about returning to Tatton Park," the captain said as he saw the two women enter the room.

"The older members of our company are returning in carriages to Tatton Park for the night. The younger people and Mrs Cooper are remaining here until the morning when the chief constable shall return with some officers to conduct a thorough search of the woods for the missing woman and two gentlemen," the Brigadier explained.

"I will remain here with Mrs Cooper. She will need some company," the countess said firmly.

"There is fog on the roads now, and the company are tired. Some of the villagers have agreed to bring some carriages from the village, and the Brigadier has put all of his carriages at our disposal," the chief constable said.

"The carriages are ready as soon as the ladies and gentlemen are," Constable Evans confirmed.

The chief constable went round to the older ladies and gentlemen and had Constable Evans escort them to the carriages in groups. Each group had no more than six members as none of the carriages could hold more than that.

Eventually, only the younger men and women were left in the drawing room along with a handful of men that had chosen to stay behind in case anything else happened.

It was arranged that the drivers of the carriages would also spend the night at Tatton Park and return in the morning.

Mrs Bosworth had organised the maids, and the rooms of the house that were generally unused were prepared for their additional guests for the night.

Bosworth returned to his duties around the house, the footmen made sure that the men were comfortable in the billiard room with cigars and measures of spirits. The women were taken to the rooms that had been prepared for them, and the house became rather still.

The doctor had chosen to stay the night, along with his sons. The doctor wanted to make sure that Mr Hunter stayed in bed and rested and that Mrs Cooper and Miss Wessex were comfortable and not too distressed.

Eventually only Sarah was left in the drawing room with Constable Evans.

"What did the chief constable have to say?" Sarah asked when she was sure that they were alone.

"He wasn't too impressed, but given the situation, I think he is probably more annoyed that something like this has happened when he was present and that even he didn't see anything," Arwyn sighed.

"Does anyone know who the woman Mrs Cooper saw Daniel talking to was?" Sarah asked.

"No, nobody seems to know who she was. I don't think she was even invited to the ball," Constable Evans said with a frown.

"There was nobody missing?" Sarah sounded surprised as she spoke.

"No one, I don't know who Mrs Cooper thought she was introducing her son to, but whoever it was, she certainly wasn't the catch that Mrs Cooper imagined she was," Constable Evans said, shaking his head.

"I don't know what Mrs Cooper would consider a catch. But if no sign of any of them could be found in the forest, then surely she is someone that is from Stickleback Hollow or the local area," Sarah said.

"Possibly, but with all the leaves on the ground; it wouldn't matter if the woman was from around here. Leaves hide where people have gone through woods during autumn, only a hunter could track even the clumsiest people through the trees," Constable Evans replied.

"So then Mr Hunter is right, if we want to find Mr Cooper and Mr Taylor, then we need Alex to track them,"

Sarah sighed.

"He is, though the doctor is right that he needs to rest. The chief constable is also not happy that you went out on your own with both of the gentlemen missing. Though, if you hadn't gone out, no one would have found Mr Hunter," Arwyn said.

"Then Captain Jonnes Smith has not improved his opinion of me?" Sarah laughed slightly.

"No, but I doubt that after the first time that he crossed paths with you, he will ever change what he thinks of you," Constable Evans replied.

"Well, then I won't concern myself too much with what he thinks then," Sarah said.

"I don't think you're the kind of woman who would care what anyone thinks of you," Arwyn replied without thinking. The moment he realised what he had said, he looked horrified. Sarah saw the look on the constable's face and started to laugh.

"There is that, though I don't want to cause any unnecessary trouble for the brigadier. I have a feeling that Captain Jonnes Smith could cause a lot of problems for him if he chose to," Sarah replied.

"You're a member of the aristocracy, Captain Jonnes Smith may have power in his title and position, but you have the weight of your family names behind you. You might be a woman, but as a member of the aristocracy, you set the tone," Arwyn said.

"I should go see if everyone has settled properly," Sarah frowned. What Constable Evans had said made her feel uncomfortable.

She didn't like the way that people looked down on one another in society based on the accident of their birth. Her Ayah had told her stories of how badly some people were treated in India under the caste system.

The idea that she had more power and influence than a man like Captain Jonnes Smith or Mr Hunter because of who her parents were was something that she would never feel comfortable with. She had always judged people based on their actions and the respect they showed to others rather than who their parents were or where they were from.

Since she had discovered that her parents were not the upstanding pillars of society that she had once thought, she had been even more uncomfortable with being told that her parents' position in society gave her power.

Chapter 12

Most of the women that had retired to bed fell asleep almost straight away. The strain of the disappearance of Mr Taylor and Mr Cooper had not only been hard on Miss Wessex and Mrs Cooper. Most of the young women seemed to be distressed that Harry was missing rather than Daniel.

Though Daniel was a handsome young man, his mother ensured that nearly every woman was kept her away from her son.

Harry's parents had allowed him much more freedom, and he had taken full advantage of that freedom. Sarah sat in the billiard room and listened to Wilbraham, Edward and Thomas talking about how Mr Taylor spent most of his time touring the country, visiting with different families and attending some of the finest parties that society had to offer.

Mr Cooper, on the other hand, was kept very close to home and only attended social events that his mother was also going to.

It was almost one o'clock in the morning when they

finished talking and were retiring to bed when there was an unexpected knock at the door. Bosworth answered it to find Miss Baker in the company of Henry Cartwright.

"Bosworth, where is Constable Evans?" Miss Baker asked in a terrified voice.

"I'll fetch him for you, Miss Baker, please sit in the parlour. Can I fetch you a drink? You look most unwell," Bosworth said with concern.

"Bring her some water please, Bosworth," Mr Cartwright said as he gently led Miss Baker towards the parlour.

"What's going on, Bosworth?" Sarah asked as she stood on the stairs with a frown on her face.

"Miss Baker and Mr Cartwright are here looking for Constable Evans," Bosworth replied.

"I'll fetch the constable, where are they?" Sarah said

"In the parlour," Bosworth replied and went to fetch some water for Miss Baker. Constable Evans hadn't gone to bed; instead, he'd gone to talk to Mr Hunter. The doctor had chosen to remain and listen to the questions Constable Evans was asking, and to make sure that Mr Hunter stayed in bed.

The doctor felt it was best to go and check on Miss

Baker. When Lady Sarah, Constable Evans and Doctor Hales entered the parlour, the brigadier was there with Bosworth.

The butler had decided to fetch his master, as there should be nothing that happened under George's roof that he didn't know about. Miss Baker and Mr Cartwright were sat on one of the long sofas. Mr Cartwright was holding Miss Baker's hand. She was pale and shaking slightly, but she had managed to maintain her composure despite this.

The doctor quickly examined her and determined that other than suffering from a nasty shock, she was quite well.

"Miss Baker, what is the matter?" Constable Evans asked with a frown as he entered the parlour with Lady Sarah and Doctor Hales.

"Constable Evans, I have come to report a robbery," Miss Baker took a deep breath before she spoke. She managed to keep her voice even as she talked, but she was shaking more visibly by the time she had finished.

Mr Cartwright patted her hand reassuringly, and she flashed him a grateful smile.

"A robbery?" Constable Evans frowned. The last robbery that Arwyn had to investigate had been the break-in at Stickleback Hollow when Bosworth had been attacked.

"Yes, when Miss Baker and her sons returned home, she found that her shop had been broken into and her leather tools had been stolen," Mr Cartwright explained.

"I see. Where are your sons now?" Constable Evans asked.

"They are boarding up the shop window. It was smashed during the robbery," Mr Cartwright said.

"And why are you here with her, Henry?" the brigadier asked.

"Miss Baker sent for me," Mr Cartwright replied flatly.

"Are you sure that only your leather tools are missing?" Sarah asked. Miss Baker nodded in reply.

"I'll come and take a look around first thing in the morning, Miss Baker. I'll ask if anyone saw anything suspicious, though with Mr Cooper and Mr Taylor vanishing, it's unlikely people will remember anything," Constable Evans sighed.

"What about my leather tools?" Miss Baker asked worriedly,

"I'll send word to the pawn shops and markets in Chester, but if they only took those tools, then clearly it was someone who knew what they were looking for and had a clear reason for needing those particular tools," the constable replied.

"I understand," Miss Baker said despondently.

"I'll have Mrs Bosworth make up two beds for you, you should rest here tonight," Sarah said with concern.

"No, thank you, my lady. I need to get home to my sons," Miss Baker said in a distracted fashion.

"I'll escort her home and make sure the place is secure for the night," Mr Cartwright said warmly. Miss Baker seemed to smile slightly as Henry spoke, but the smile so briefly flickered across her lips that Sarah wondered if she had really seen it.

Bosworth and the brigadier walked Miss Baker and Mr Cartwright to the front door, and the doctor retired to bed.

"Why would anyone break into Miss Baker's shop and only steal leather tools? The leather is worth more than the tools, and there are reams of silks that she has that would fetch a good price. It doesn't make sense," Sarah frowned.

"Oh no, you are not getting involved in another burglary investigation. This is something that the Cheshire Constabulary will deal with without your very kind assistance," Arwyn warned.

"If you say so," Sarah shrugged, "I should go to bed. It's very late," she yawned.

Constable Evans narrowed his eyes as he watched the lady leave the parlour and had an uneasy feeling in his stomach that he was going to get another earful from the Chief Constable because Sarah couldn't help but investigate anything that was even marginally mysterious.

Sarah didn't retire to bed; instead, she went to see Mr Hunter. He was sat up as she entered the room.

"What brought Miss Baker back here?" Alex asked as Sarah sat down beside the bed.

"Someone broke into her shop and stole her leather tools," Sarah was still frowning and bit her lip as she spoke.

"Are you all right?" Alex asked.

"How long has the doctor said you need to rest for?" Sarah asked.

"A few days. He says my body needs chance to recover. If I don't stay in bed, he's threatened to have me taken to the Manchester Royal Infirmary," Alex sighed, "You didn't answer my question."

"You said before that there was no particular reason that you were at Swallow's End when I found you," Sarah said slowly.

"I did," Alex agreed.

"I don't believe you," Sarah said, looking at Alex with a fixed stare.

"That isn't my concern," Alex tried to shrug and winced instead.

"There are too many dark and strange things happening around here tonight – Miss Baker is robbed, Harry and Daniel go missing, a woman screams in the forest and vanishes without a trace, you are injured riding on the Grangeback estate – something is going on, and I intend to find out what," Sarah said with fire in her eyes.

"I think you are connecting events that are completely disassociated from one another," Alex said sternly.

"I think you're wrong, and since you won't tell me why you were at Swallow's End, I have no choice but to find out what is going on for myself," Sarah said firmly. She stood without another word and left the room. Alex lay back on his pillows and sighed.

There was nothing he could do to stop her, and even if she was locked in her rooms, she would simply climb out of the window. Alex silently cursed the beasts that had attacked him and caused him to be confined to his bed. As long as he was injured, he couldn't protect Sarah,s and he had the uneasy feeling that she was heading into more danger than she realised.

Chapter 13

Grangeback was oddly silent as Sarah walked down the stairs. Sarah had imagined that the number of people staying in the house that night would create more noise, even when sleeping, but it was as quiet as any other night.

Constable Evans, Mr Moore, Mr Walker, Wilbraham, Thomas and Edward were all still awake. Stuart and Jake had volunteered to stay up in case Daniel and Harry returned to the house. Wilbraham was used to long periods of time without sleep, so he had wandered around Grangeback several times, checking that everything was secure, before joining Jake and Stuart in the billiard room.

Thomas and Edward were concerned for their friends. Charlotte and Mary had chosen to spend the night with Elizabeth, neither woman wanted to leave their friend on her own when she was so distraught. The brothers had tried to sleep, but after lying in darkness for a frustrating half an hour, they had both given up and come back down to the billiard room.

Constable Evans was concerned about the break-in at Miss Baker's shop and his mind mulling over what Sarah had said about the leather and silk being far more valuable than the tools that were stolen.

Despite the number of people awake in the early hours of the morning, the house was still as Sarah went down to the kitchen. She was trying to figure out a connection between all the unusual events of the night or whether Mr Hunter was right and none of the things were connected.

Cooky had left the fire burning in the stove so that Mr Walker and Mr Moore would be able to make tea whilst the household staff were asleep.

Sarah filled the kettle and placed it on the stove before going to sit in Cooky's chair. She sighed to herself and rubbed her temples. The water didn't have a chance to boil before Sarah was distracted from her thoughts by the hurried tramp of feet approaching the kitchen.

Wilbraham, Thomas, Edward, Arwyn, Stuart and Jake came rushing into the kitchen with concerned expressions on their faces.

"What is it?" Sarah asked as she looked from one man to the next.

"The dogs that attacked Hunter, they are running around the house," Thomas said gravely.

"You saw them?" Sarah leapt to her feet as she spoke.

"They ran past the windows and threw themselves at the doors. I think they are trying to find some way of getting into the house," Edward replied.

An ear-splitting screech cut through whatever would have been said next. It was the sound a terrified horse in a small space.

"The horses!" Sarah cried. She didn't think at all, but rushed to the door, undid the bolts and the lock and sprinted out into the night before any of the men could react. She was only a few steps away from the backdoor, whereas the men were on the other side of the kitchen.

Sarah ran through the night. She fumbled with the string tie on her purse that still hung at her waist, as she tried to get out her pistol. If she had stopped to think for a moment, she might have had the chance to be frightened.

Mr Hunter, a man that was more adept at hunting animals and living in the English countryside than Sarah would ever be, had been left half-dead by these dogs. But Sarah had spent her youth in India, walking through forests that leopards and tigers called home.

In her mind, dogs were nothing compared to the big cats of India, but then Sarah had never faced feral dogs or wolves before and didn't know the terror that a chorus of howls could instil in the hearts of men in remote places when deep winter snows had lasted too long, and the beasts were hungry.

The sounds of Harald and Black Guy in distress caused Sarah to run as fast as she could. She tripped and stumbled a few times in the dark since she hadn't paused to take a lantern before tearing off towards the stables.

When she finally reached the stables, she couldn't see a thing in the darkness. She could hear the horses panicking, kicking at their stable doors, but she also heard a sound that terrified her so deeply that she was frozen to the spot.

It was the sound of soft padding on wet earth. It was so quiet that it would have almost gone completely unnoticed due to the racquet the horses were making, but it was a slight noise that caused Sarah's ears to prick. It was the sound of something hunting her. A predator that was moving slowly and purposefully in the darkness. It wasn't just one anima either.

The hairs on her arms all stood up on end as she screwed up her eyes in terror and strained her ears to focus on the sound of the padding. She couldn't tell how far away the beasts were, only that they were close. They could smell her, and even if she chose to turn and run back to the house now, she would never make it.

Fear rose in her chest and threatened to overwhelm her as she stood there. Her hand clutched tightly at the pistol, but with no light, she had no way of knowing where to shoot. She thought about firing a shot at the sky to try and scare off the animals, but she had no way of knowing if that would work or would simply cause the predators to attack.

Then the growling started. A deep guttural sound that made Sarah want to whimper in fear. The growling told her that the dogs were much closer than she had imagined, and this realisation was the final trigger. She fired the gun wildly into the dark, hoping to hit something. She missed, but as the sound of her shot rang out, it was suddenly joined by the sound of other guns firing.

The dogs yelped and ran off as Wilbraham, Edward, Thomas, Stuart and Jake all fired muskets. Constable Evans carried a lantern that threw a large circle of light, showing the men where Sarah was and where the dogs had been.

When the men were sure that the dogs had run off, they stopped firing.

"My lady, are you all right?" Constable Evans asked as he walked over to where Sarah was rooted to the spot. The moment that Arwyn saw Sarah's face, he knew that she wasn't all right. Her eyes were clamped tightly shut, and tears were rolling down her cheeks.

Without a word, Wilbraham stepped over to Sarah and scooped her up in his arms and carried her back to the house. The other men followed behind, making sure that the dogs didn't return. The house was secured again, and Sarah was carried to Mr Hunter's room.

Alex had barely survived an attack by those dogs, Harry and Daniel were missing in the woods that the three creatures were prowling and Wilbraham wanted to know all he could about the beasts before he set out to hunt them down. Wild dogs were too dangerous to be left roaming the countryside with winter so close to setting in.

Chapter 14

Thomas and Edward went to fetch the brigadier and Doctor Hales as Sarah was carried up the stairs by Wilbraham. The young lady hadn't said a word as she was brought in from the stables.

Mr Hunter wasn't asleep as Constable Evans opened the door to his room and brought Sarah in.

"What happened?" Alex asked as he tried to get out of bed.

"Three dogs were at the stables trying to attack the horses, her ladyship went out to try and save them," Wilbraham explained as he lay Sarah down on the chaise lounge in the corner of the room.

"Is she all right? Did they hurt her?" Alex demanded as he struggled across the room to kneel next to Sarah.

"No, they didn't. We went after her. If we'd arrived much later, they might have," Constable Evans sighed.

"I'm going to go and help Mr Moore and Mr Walker check the rest of the house is secure and that nothing managed to get in whilst we were out," Wilbraham excused himself from the room as George and Jack arrived.

"Sarah! What on earth were you thinking?" George demanded. The old soldier was clearly angry with the young lady, but the pallor of her skin checked the rage in his voice.

"She's not hurt, George, just shock. It might be best to let her rest where she is. Mr Hunter, why are you out of bed?" the doctor shouted at Alex, his eyebrows knitted together.

"Because -" Mr Hunter began, but he was cut off by the doctor.

"No excuses! Back to bed, or so help me, I'll make sure you're taken to the hospital for a month!" Jack said sternly.

"We should take Sarah to her room to rest," George said as he reached out to take Sarah's hand.

"Let her rest where she is, as long as she is in the room, Mr Hunter might just stay in his bed and rest. No harm will come to her here," the doctor replied to the brigadier.

"Very well, what an evening this is turning into. It was supposed to be another dull ball, but instead all of this," George sighed, shaking his head.

"They say that on All Hallows' Eve evil forces stalk the land because the veil between the spirit world and ours is at its weakest," the doctor shrugged.

"Did I just hear superstition from a man of medicine?" the brigadier derisively teased his friend.

"I am merely repeating the ramblings of others. I never said I believed it. The number of people that were all in the same place tonight, something was bound to go wrong," the doctor said defensively.

"Possibly, but all of this seems a little much to me," George frowned.

"Well, if you'll all excuse me, I should be returning to my bed. I would like to get at least an hours rest before the sun rises," the doctor said gruffly and left George to help Alex back to his bed.

Sarah had closed her eyes and seemed to have fallen asleep; the shock of being surrounded by three dogs in the darkness had clearly taken its toll on her nerves.

"I think I'm headed for an early grave," George said as he half-carried Alex back to bed.

"What makes you say that?" Alex asked.

"Between your reckless behaviour and my ward running headlong into danger, I think the worry might just kill me," George said pointedly as Alex gingerly lay down.

"You'll outlive us all," Alex smiled as George pulled the covers over the hunter.

"In the case of both of you, that might just be true," George replied tartly.

"Sarah is fine, George. She wasn't on her own," Alex soothed.

"No, but you were. What on earth were you doing riding around in the dead of night like that?" George demanded in a hushed tone.

"I wasn't riding around at night on my own. I was there for a day and a night before Sarah found me," Alex said and then wished he hadn't spoken.

"You were lying out there, dying for over a day before you were found?" George hissed.

"It's not as bad as it sounds," Alex insisted.

"What am going to do with you both? Why were you there in the first place?" George asked.

"There were signs of strange things in the forest. Things were being moved, and there were animal tracks that shouldn't have been there. So I followed the tracks and ended up at Swallow's End," Alex explained.

"Where you were attacked," George huffed.

"There were three dogs, bigger than I've ever seen before. They looked more like wolves than dogs, but they didn't move or hunt in quite the same way," Alex said.

"They could be Akitas then," George said, rubbing his chin.

"Akitas?" Alex frowned.

"They are an oriental hunting dog. They are big and look like wolves, though not quite as sleek," George replied.

"You've come across them before?" Alex asked.

"Yes, they come from Japan. I was there before Lucy was born. Some of the Emperor's men took us out hunting with them. They were terrifying to behold as hunting animals," George said.

"So why would they be here now?" Alex asked.

"I don't know. Though for dogs like that to be running around in the forest, someone would have had to put them there," George yawned and sat down in the chair beside Alex's bed.

"Do they normally attack people?" Alex asked.

"It depends on what is being hunted," George pursed his lips, and Alex felt his stomach jolt.

"I walked into a trap," Mr Hunter said, staring at the

foot of the bed in disbelief.

"A trap?" George frowned.

"I was drawn up to Swallows' End by the unusual trail and then was struck down when I was alone up there. I was left for dead in a place hardly anyone ever visits," Alex said slowly.

"Except Sarah," George added.

"Except Sarah," Alex agreed.

"You think that they intended for Sarah to find you dead?" George asked.

"Yes, and now Harry and Daniel have disappeared," Alex said as he leant his head back against the headboard and closed his eyes.

"You think that's related?" George asked.

"Daniel's mother has been telling everyone for weeks that Sarah has designs on her son and that she will not countenance any union between them. They met once, but Ruth Cooper -"

"Yes, she's a woman possessed of a rather singular vision," George said delicately.

"And Harry will have been telling everyone who will listen that he's met the infamous Lady Sarah Montgomery

Baird Watson-Wentworth and what a rare and exotic woman she is," Alex continued.

"Which has attracted the attention of one John Smith," George gave a heavy sigh and shook his head.

"You said she has spies everywhere, she'll know that I helped Sarah stop her from getting that pocket watch," Alex said quietly.

"And she'll have heard about Daniel and Harry having a connection to her as well. Did you hide the pocket watch?" George asked.

"Yes, no one will find it unless I tell them where it is," Alex replied.

"Good. I'm going to go and see what state my household is in after all this. You should try and get some sleep. Sarah's too exhausted after the ordeal to go anywhere," George sighed.

"Do you think the dogs would have attacked her?" Alex asked.

"If John Smith sent them, no, they would have either kept her there until someone came for her or taken her back to their master," George said thoughtfully.

"Then there is no need to chide her for rushing out to

save the horses," Alex gave George a wry smile.

"I wish the two of you would be less reckless," George sighed and left the room. Alex settled back on his pillows and closed his eyes. It didn't take long for him to fall asleep, and as he started to snore, Sarah opened her eyes.

She slowly sat up and hugged her knees to her chest. If she really was the reason that Alex was injured and that Daniel and Harry were now missing, then she was going to be the person to find them.

Chapter 15

Sarah trod as quietly as she could to the door. She had to step softly and walk slowly so that she didn't wake Alex. She didn't know whether Mr Hunter was a light sleeper or not, but she couldn't risk waking him.

When she reached the door, she placed her hand against the door and slowly pulled it open. It creaked noisily, and Sarah cringed. She glanced nervously at Alex, but fortunately, he hadn't woken up. He didn't even stir at the sound of the creaking door.

Sarah slipped soundlessly out into the hallway. She shut the door carefully behind her and glanced up and down the corridor before she moved towards the stairs.

She knew that Mr Moore and Mr Walker were both still awake downstairs with the brigadier and Constable Evans. She didn't know whether they would be waiting for the morning in the billiard room or whether they would be patrolling the house.

Sarah decided that it was best to not risk being seen by

taking the main staircase, but the servants' stairs were unlikely to be used or even watched at this time in the morning. The only person that might be using them what would be awake was Bosworth, though Sarah was certain that if Bosworth hadn't gone back to bed, he would be wherever the Brigadier was.

If the hounds that were prowling around in the woods were there for her, then they wouldn't go until they had found her. She went down to the kitchen and took one of the lanterns. She made sure that it was lit before she unlocked the door and slipped out into the night, making sure to lock the door behind her again.

She didn't head to the stables as she normally would for going into the woods. She didn't want to risk either of the horses. Having seen what the dogs had done to Alex and how he had been left for dead, she was certain that the dogs would kill whichever mount she took.

She held the lantern firmly in her left hand as she walked down the path that led away from the house, and grasped her pistol firmly in her right hand.

Sarah was careful to keep the lantern low so it would be less likely to be seen from the house, just in case anyone happened to look out of the window. It seemed to take hours to cross the lawns and make it into the trees. In reality, it was more like twenty minutes, but Sarah was so tense that time seemed to stretch to endless proportions.

The forest was oddly still. Normally there were the sounds of birds twittering and animals scurrying about, even at night there were the sounds of life that were oddly comforting.

Now there was nothing. The only sound Sarah could hear were the leaves crunching underneath her feet as she walked.

The sound seemed to be magnified in the unnatural stillness. She knew that there was no way for her to track anything through the forest, but she didn't need to. What she needed to find was signs of whoever the dogs belonged to.

No one had seen any signs of the dogs before Alex had been attacked, and there had been no sign of them around the grounds afterwards. This meant they had to be hiding somewhere, and the only place that Sarah knew of in the woods where the dogs and their master could hide was the lodge where Mr Hunter lived.

Sarah doubted that Alex had been attacked because of

his association with her. He was a man without standing in society and could do very little against the type of machinations that Sarah believed her parents had been involved with alongside the mysterious John Smith.

The only reason Sarah could think of that Alex would be attacked and left for dead in a remote part of the grounds was that they needed his home to hide in.

As she walked through the woods, she kept her eyes open for dogs and strained her ears to make sure that no one was sneaking up on her. But as anxious as she felt, her mind kept wandering back to John Smith.

When she had been lying on the chaise lounge in Alex's room George and Alex had referred to John Smith as a she. Both of them knew more than they were prepared to tell her about John Smith, and this both annoyed and upset Sarah.

There was nothing that could be gained from getting distracted by questions about John Smith, and why Mr Hunter and the brigadier were keeping her in the dark.

There was nothing moving in the forest, and Sarah started to relax slightly as she walked. It took her less time than she thought it would to reach the lodge.

There were no lights on, but there was a thick covering

116

of leaves by the door that had been trodden down, something that looked very out of place at the home of a hunter who always used the backdoor and rarely had visitors.

Sarah quietly circled round to the back of the house. She lifted the latch on the door and slipped inside, careful to make as little noise as she could.

There were no lanterns lit in the house, aside from the one that Sarah carried. As soon as she put the lantern on the table, she could see that there everything was out of place, but the dogs and whoever commanded them weren't there.

She felt relieved that she hadn't stumbled across them all at the same time, but frustrated that she still didn't know who was behind all the strange goings-on.

Chapter 16

Just because there was no one there now, didn't mean that they wouldn't be coming back. Sarah knew that she didn't have an infinite amount of time to look around the lodge to try and find out who it was she was looking for and if they really were working for John Smith. She also knew that moving anything was a bad idea.

The slightest thing out of place would tell whoever was out there that someone had found their hiding place and Sarah didn't want to force their hand.

She picked up the lantern and used the light to guide her path through all the disarray around her. There were papers strewn across the floor, furniture had been moved from its normal place, and there were clothes scattered about the room.

Some of them Sarah recognised as Alex's clothes, but the others looked like they belonged to a woman. Sarah paused and frowned as she tried to examine the clothes without touching them. They didn't look old, so probably didn't belong to Mr Hunter's mother.

She didn't linger too long to think about whose they might be. Instead, she walked towards the stairs and ascended to the floor above. The lodge wasn't very big. There was the sitting area and kitchen downstairs and two bedrooms upstairs. It wasn't anything particularly special, but Mr Hunter kept it in very good condition.

One of the bedrooms had belonged to his mother when she had been alive, and it had largely remained untouched since her death. As far as Sarah knew, she was the only person to have used the room since Emma Hunter had died.

The other room belonged to Mr Hunter. It wasn't particularly well-furnished, not for want of wealth, but because function matter to Alex more than aesthetics did.

There was nothing on the stairs for Sarah to disturb as she climbed, so she didn't have to worry about tripping or knocking anything as she moved. However, she was wary about making too much noise, just in case the dogs and their master were sleeping upstairs.

She walked to Emma's room first and slowly opened the door. The room was empty and didn't seem to be in disarray like the rooms downstairs. She closed the door behind her as she left and went to check on Alex's room.

The door creaked open as she gingerly pushed it and stuck her head into the room. There were no dogs in the room. Instead, the figures of Mr Taylor and Mr Cooper lay on the floor.

Their hands were bound and their mouths gagged, but they were otherwise unhurt. As soon as Sarah saw the two men, she flung the door to one side and rushed into the room.

"Daniel!" Sarah cried as she dropped to her knees, put down the lantern and pulled the gag out of Daniel's mouth.

"Sarah? What are you doing here?" Daniel demanded as Sarah pulled the piece of cloth down from his mouth and moved to do the same for Harry.

"I came looking for you. All the men from Stickleback Hollow and the ball have been out looking for you." Sarah replied.

"Where are they now?" Harry asked.

"They've stopped for the night; they couldn't find any sign of you in the woods. They were going to start again in the morning," Sarah said as she tried to undo the ropes around Harry's wrists.

"Not even Hunter could track us in the woods?"

Daniel frowned.

"He was missing too. I found him at Swallows' End. He'd been attacked by big dogs and left for dead in the trees," Sarah explained.

"Is he all right?" Harry asked with concern.

"He's alive and at Grangeback. The doctor has told him to rest, but he doesn't seem to be in any danger," Sarah replied.

"If Hunter is being forced to rest and the men have all stopped looking for the night, who came out here with you?" Daniel demanded to know as he struggled to try and kneel.

"No one, I came on my own," Sarah shrugged.

"You came out here on your own? After you found Hunter half-dead in the forest?" Daniel asked with disbelief.

"And after I met the dogs that attacked him," Sarah said with a deadpan expression.

Daniel blinked and didn't quite know what to say next to the lady.

"I can't untie these knots. They're too tight," Sarah said with frustration.

"Do you have a knife? You could try cutting the ropes," Harry suggested.

"No, she needs to go back to Grangeback and get help. My lady, you need to leave here before they come back. They are here for you. They've been asking us questions about you. You need to go back to Grangeback and stay there. Don't leave the house; send the others to come get us," Daniel said urgently.

"What are you talking about? Who are they?" Sarah asked.

"I don't know. My mother introduced me to one of them as the niece of Mr and Mrs Mullaney, but the name she gave my mother isn't the name she is using now. I don't know what her real name is," Daniel replied.

"There's more than one of them?" Sarah asked with a knitted brow.

"Sarah, behind you!" Harry shouted.

Sarah turned to see a woman dressed in black clothing that was more at home in the Orient than in the heart of the Cheshire countryside. She had a gun in her hand that she was aiming square at Sarah's chest.

Sarah barely had the chance to realise what she was faced with before the gun in the woman's hand, fired. The bullet cracked into Sarah's shoulder. She screamed as pain exploded across her shoulder and she dropped her own pistol. She felt the warm flow of blood over her skin as she fell to the floor.

The force of the bullet hitting her shoulder had knocked her backwards so that she fell over Daniel and cracked her head hard on the edge of Alex's bed.

A slight groan escaped her lips as she slumped to the floor. The woman with the gun stuffed it into the silk sash that was tied around her waist and walked over to where Sarah lay.

Daniel and Harry both shouted at the woman and called Sarah's name, but Sarah was unconscious, and the mysterious woman ignored them.

Chapter 17

Constable Evans sighed and looked at his pocket watch. It showed that it was 3 o'clock in the morning. It felt like the night had lasted for an eternity already. Arwyn sighed to himself as he closed the watch and slipped it back into his pocket.

There was no one moving in the house. It had been still since they had brought Sarah in from the stables. The brigadier had retired to bed an hour after Sarah had fallen asleep in Mr Hunter's room.

There was no reason for him to stay up when Constable Evans, Mr Walker and Mr Moore were all awake. Arwyn had agreed to check on Sarah every few hours.

The policeman walked along the corridor. He wasn't too concerned about waking people up with his walking – most were too exhausted to wake up at the sound of his footsteps. Those that were woken would soon fall back to sleep again.

He knocked gently on the door of Mr Hunter's room

before he entered. Alex stirred in his bed at the sound of knocking, but didn't wake up. He had lost a lot of blood, and now that he was in a warm bed, had his injuries treated, had been given food and fluid, he was finally asleep.

It would take more than a soft knock on the door to wake him. But Constable Evans wasn't knocking on the door for Mr Hunter's sake. It was for Lady Sarah's.

It took a few moments for Arwyn's eyes to adjust to the darkness in the room. The lamp next to Alex's bed had been extinguished, and Constable Evans hadn't brought a lamp with him. The lamps in the corridor had been left on a low light for the men to use to navigate the house so they wouldn't need to carry their own.

Arwyn made his way to the table beside Mr Hunter's bed and lit it. He kept the light low enough not to disturb Alex, but just high enough that he could see the chaise in the corner of the room.

Constable Evans frowned and rubbed his eyes. The chaise lounge was empty. He half-sprinted around to the chaise, just in case his tired eyes were playing tricks on him. But as he reached the chaise, he could see and feel that it was empty.

Arwyn swore and cursed loudly, jolting Alex out of his slumber.

"Sarah?" Mr Hunter called out as he woke up and looked wildly around the room.

"She's not here," Arwyn said with frustration.

"Arwyn?" Alex asked, rubbing his eyes with his good arm.

"Yes, Mr Hunter," Arwyn sighed.

"Where is Lady Sarah?" Alex asked as he managed to shake the cobwebs from his mind.

"I don't know, but I need to find out," Constable Evans sighed.

Arwyn stormed out of Alex's room and went to find Mr Walker and Mr Moore. Between the three of them, the men searched the house from top to bottom. They opened the door of every room and woke everyone up in an effort to find Lady Sarah. By the time it was clear that Sarah was not in Grangeback, the whole house was awake.

"First, my son goes missing, and now that wretched girl. Now can you see it was all her doing?" Mrs Cooper demanded as she stood in the corridor and tried to find someone who would listen to her.

"Mrs Bosworth, would you be so kind as to take Mrs Cooper back to bed?" the brigadier asked in a loud voice that told everyone who heard it that it was not a request but an order.

Mrs Bosworth took Mrs Cooper by the arm and marched her back to her room.

"If you are certain that she is no longer in the house, then I would suggest a search party be formed. There are enough young men in the house to send," the countess said with authority.

"I'm going to look for her," Alex announced as he tried to weave his way down the corridor. Even with his bandaged and useless shoulder, Mr Hunter had managed to climb out of bed, dress himself and stagger down to where people were congregating in the hall.

"Mr Hunter, go back to bed this instant!" the doctor ordered, but Alex stood his ground.

"Mr Cooper and Mr Taylor being missing is one thing, but Lady Sarah being missing is another," Mr Hunter insisted.

"George, send the boy back to bed. There are enough young men here to search for her," Doctor Hales appealed to the brigadier for help.

127

"No, Jack, with Sarah missing, I want Mr Hunter searching for her with the rest of us," George said, shaking his head.

"Bosworth and the doctor should remain at the house with the older footmen and the men. Everyone else come to the kitchen as soon as you are dressed. The brigadier will divide the grounds for us to search. As soon as three or more men have assembled to form a small search party, they can be sent out by the brigadier to search. Once you have searched the area, come back to the house," Constable Evans instructed.

The men nodded and disappeared back to their rooms. The women gathered together and started to mumble to one another. George, Bosworth, Jack, Alex and Arwyn made their way down to the kitchen.

"I need to go to the lodge to get some weapons and equipment," Mr Hunter said as they stepped into the heart of the house.

"Constable Evans will go with you; the two of you can start searching the forest on the edge of the estate for any signs of Sarah," the brigadier said.

"We'll need to go through the front door until Bosworth can find the spare key," Alex said to Arwyn.

"Why can't we use the backdoor?" Constable Evans frowned as he went to take the key from its hook.

"You didn't know that Sarah wasn't in the house, the only way she could have gotten out of the house unnoticed is through that door," Alex gave Arwyn a wry smile.

"She took the key and locked it behind her," Arwyn said with surprise.

"Bosworth, the spare key please, Jack, show Mr Hunter and Constable Evans out of the front door if you would be so kind," the brigadier said as he sat down to split his land into sections to be searched.

Mr Hunter and Constable Evans went out the front door and across the grounds towards the lodge.

As they walked, Arwyn carried a lantern to light their way, Alex scanned the ground, looking for signs of Sarah, but also Daniel, Harry, the dogs that had attacked him and the mysterious woman that had screamed in the woods.

"She came this way," Mr Hunter said as they got closer to the trees.

"You're sure?" Arwyn asked as he looked at the ground, trying to see what Alex could see.

"Yes, it looks like she went to the lodge," Alex replied.

The two men followed the trail that Sarah had left. When they got closer to the lodge, Alex stopped again to examine the ground.

"The dogs have been here quite a lot. Not recently though. Sarah's tracks go over theirs. There's the trail of another woman here too. Daniel and Harry have been here as well," Alex said.

"Do you think there is anyone still inside?" Arwyn asked.

"We'll soon find out," Alex replied and led the way round to the back of the lodge. The two men entered the lodge the same way Sarah had. They saw the same disruption to Alex's belongings that Sarah had seen.

"Don't touch anything," Mr Hunter instructed and led Arwyn to the stairs. Alex followed the path that Sarah had taken through the lodge, doing his best to make as little noise as possible.

As the two men reached the top of the stairs, Alex opened the door to his mother's room to check that everything was where it should be. When he was satisfied that nothing was out of place, the two men turned their attention to Mr Hunter's room.

"Hunter? Thank God, it's you," Daniel said with relief as he laid his eyes on his school friend.

"What happened here?" Constable Evans asked as he went to untie Daniel and Harry. But Alex stood in the doorway, staring at dark circles on the floor.

"Whose blood is that?" he asked as he stared at the patches of fresh splatter that coated the floor.

"It's Sarah's. The bitch shot her," Daniel replied bitterly.

The blood instantly drained from Alex's face, and he felt as weak as he had when he lay dying from his wounds at Swallows' End.

"What happened?" Arwyn asked.

Between the two of them, Harry and Daniel explained how they had been taken into the woods by the woman that Mrs Cooper had introduced Daniel to and how another two women and the three dogs had been waiting for them. They told Alex and Arwyn how Sarah had found them and what had happened when the woman came back.

"Is Sarah alive?" Alex asked at the end of the story.

"I don't know, but before the woman took Sarah away, she was asking her about poppies," Harry replied.

"Poppies?" Arwyn frowned.

"Papaver somniferum," Daniel replied.

"Opium poppies," Alex said, shaking his head.

"Do you know what this is all about?" Daniel asked.

"No," Alex said flatly, "Arwyn, take Mr Cooper and Mr Taylor back to Grangeback. I'm going to look for Sarah."

The hunter moved round to the far side of his bed and pulled a trunk out from under it. He took out his Howdah pistol along with his bow and quiver.

Chapter 18

"You can't go on your own," Arwyn replied.

"I'm coming with you," Daniel said as the constable managed to free the young gentleman's hands.

"Your mother is worried. You need to go back to the house," Alex argued.

"I'll go back to the house. I'll tell them what happened." Harry offered.

"Mr Taylor going back alone makes more sense than you going after Lady Sarah and her kidnappers on your own," Arwyn agreed.

"As you wish," Alex relented.

Mr Hunter went to search the surrounding area for signs of where the women had gone. There were some blood drops through the lodge that he could easily follow, but there had been no signs outside that he had seen when they approached.

"Someone will need to be sent from Grangeback to fetch the Chief Constable from Tatton Park," Arwyn told

Harry as the policeman stood watching him untie his feet.

"I'll tell the brigadier. He'll know who to send," Harry said.

When both Daniel and Harry were free, the two men staggered to their feet and tried to walk. They had been tied up for hours and lying in the same position, so both men struggled with dead limbs and pins and needles for a few minutes before they were able to walk properly.

By the time both Daniel and Harry had made it down the stairs, Alex had returned to the lodge. He had found a faint blood trail as well as signs that at least two women had gone deeper into the woods.

"I will see you back at Grangeback," Harry said goodbye to the three men and set off into the early morning.

"Did you find anything?" Daniel asked Alex.

"They're headed to the Edge. It's a difficult climb at night. You should change into something less formal," Alex replied.

The hunter gave Mr Cooper some of his older hunting clothes that were too small for the giant man and a pair of boots that would make tracking through the trees and up the difficult slope much easier.

Whilst Daniel changed, Constable Evans and Mr Hunter collected lanterns and hunting weapons from around the lodge.

Arwyn was left to trim the wicks and light the lanterns as well as to check the weapons, the powder and shot. Alex went around the room to collect the papers off the floor, sort through his clothes and the clothes that the woman had left on the floor.

He wasn't simply trying to tidy up his home, he was looking for clues. Every piece of paper he picked up, he scanned, looking for some mention of who the women were and if there was any link between them and Lady Carol-Ann Margaret de Mandeville.

There was nothing that he could see that provided any answers, but when he found Sarah and the woman that had shot her, he would make sure that he found out something.

By the time Daniel had changed and come down to the kitchen, Arwyn had prepared the guns, and the lanterns and Alex had cleared most of the debris from the floor.

The three men set off into the night carrying a Baker rifle each and a lantern. Mr Hunter also had his Howdah pistol tucked into his belt. It was a heavy weapon, but one that would be of far more use at close range than his rifle. Alex also had a bow and arrow slung across his back.

The hunter preferred the bow to using a gun when it came to hunting and carried it now out of habit rather than necessity.

He led the way through the trees, the pace set at a light jog, something that the hunter hoped that Daniel and Arwyn would both be able to maintain over the flat ground.

As they skirted around the edge of the village, the ground started to rise, telling the men that they had come to the start of the Edge. Alex slowed down to a walk, but it was still a brisk pace as he started his ascent.

Constable Evans was struggling to keep up with the hunter, but Mr Cooper was exhausted and ready to collapse. The young gentleman considered himself to be active, but it was nothing compared to what Mr Hunter did.

Daniel didn't complain as they slowed down, and he tried to catch his breath. Alex was moving ahead of the other two men, following the trail until he had to stop and search for where the two women had gone.

"What is it?" Arwyn asked as he caught up with the hunter.

"She's stopped bleeding. There haven't been any blood splatters from a while now, but it looks like they are heading to the druid site," Alex replied, shaking his head.

"The druid site?" Daniel frowned. He'd never heard of anything like that in the area.

"It's an abandoned site on the top of the Edge. People used to gather there and conduct ceremonies on All Hallows' Eve. It's supposed to be a spiritual focal point of the area. Before I was born, the brigadier and some of the men from the Stickleback and from Tatton went and cleared the site. Anyone that went there was taken by the night watchmen and forced to leave the area. Since then, no one has used it," Alex explained.

"How can you be sure no one has been using it?" Arwyn asked.

"Part of the groundskeeper duties at Grangeback is to check the Edge for signs of druids using the site," Alex replied.

His shoulder was still troubling him, and the fast pace that he had set moving to the Edge had left him feeling light-headed.

"How far are we from the druid site?" Daniel asked.

"Quite a way, it's right on the top plateau, and worse

137

still, those dogs have been here too. There are more tracks than Sarah's and the woman's too. We need to keep our eyes open," Alex warned as he stood up. He felt the blood rush away from his head and almost blacked out.

"Are you all right?" Constable Evans frowned.

"I'll be fine, come on, we've got a long way to go, and it's going to be light in a few hours," Alex replied.

Chapter 19

It took the three men almost an hour to reach the top of the Edge. Alex slowed them to a crawling pace as he spotted a fire through the trees.

They stopped a good twenty feet from where the fire was and waited whilst Alex assessed the situation. Sarah was lying on the ground by the fire, she was tied up, and the dried blood could be seen on her clothes. Her skin looked pale in the firelight, and her eyes were closed.

There were three women sat around the fire. They didn't seem at all concerned with Sarah's condition but seemed to be chanting something.

"Do you know who they are?" Constable Evans whispered.

"The one with blonde hair is Alison Moore, she's Stuart's sister, I don't know why she would be out here. Jane Beech is the brown-haired girl. She was engaged to Harry a few years ago, but her father was given a job with the East India Company, and they moved to London. The red-haired

139

girl is the one my mother introduced me to, Miss Annabel Turner," Daniel said as he pointed to each of the women in turn.

"What are they wearing?" Constable Evans frowned. Each of the women was dressed in black silks that Mr Cooper had seen before.

"They're clothes from Japan, typically worn by an extinct order called shinobi. They're more of a mythical legend now than fact," Daniel explained.

"I would have thought their clothes were from China," Arwyn frowned.

"The silks might well be, but the style isn't," Daniel replied.

"That explains the Akitas then," Alex sighed and shook his head.

"What do we do?" Daniel asked.

"We go and get Sarah back. I doubt that the women can fight. They might be armed, but we have the element of surprise, and the dogs don't seem to be anywhere close at hand," Mr Hunter said firmly.

He stood up and walked forward with his Howdah pistol drawn. He had thought about unslinging his rifle, but at close range the Howdah would do more damage.

"Mr Hunter, still alive?" Miss Beech asked as she gracefully rose to her feet. Alex hadn't tried to hide his approach, and the moment that the women heard his footsteps, they had stopped chanting.

"You should never leave a man for dead, unless you want him to come looking for you," Alex replied bitterly.

"Well then, this time, we'll make sure that you've gone to meet your maker before we leave," Miss Turner smiled maliciously as she stepped away from the fire and took a few steps towards Sarah.

Alex fired the pistol, and Annabel stopped dead in her steps.

"You should be careful with that thing, you might hurt someone," Alison said with a touch of condescension.

"You stay away from Lady Sarah," Mr Hunter said firmly.

"If you hadn't come alone, then maybe you would have been able to stop us, but as it is, you are injured and outnumbered," Jane grinned.

"He didn't come alone," Arwyn said as he stepped forward, aiming the Baker rifle at the women. Daniel was beside him, doing the same thing. The women were momentarily distracted, and Alex took the opportunity to slip his pistol into his belt and drawn the bow from his back.

It was excruciatingly painful as he raised the bow and took an arrow from his quiver. Constable Evans could see the pain etched on the face of Alex as he drew back the bowstring.

Moving his shoulder to shrug had left him almost unconscious a few hours before, but now he was drawing back on his bow and gritting his teeth to try and counter the pain he was in.

"You should have brought more men," Annabel replied smugly. She raised her pistol and aimed it at Alex. Before she could fire, Mr Hunter released his bowstring, and the arrow snapped into Miss Turner's shoulder.

As Annabel fell, Jane whistled. Daniel and Arwyn looked wildly around as the sound of barking filled the air. A few seconds later, the three large hunting dogs from Japan leapt from the trees. Constable Evans and Mr Cooper both fired their rifles. Two of the dogs dropped to the ground, one was dead, and the other was whining in pain.

The third dog ran and jumped at Alex. The beast was snarling, and its teeth came dangerously close to ripping into the hunter's throat. Alex used his bow to keep the dog from biting him, but with the pain in his shoulder and his loss of blood; he wasn't strong enough to push the dog off.

When Arwyn was sure that the other two dogs weren't going to attack, he ran over and hit the one attacking Alex with the butt of his rifle. The dog fell to the ground and didn't get up again.

Alex's rifle lay on the ground beside him; it had been knocked from his shoulder by the force of the dog landing on him. The constable picked it up and aimed it at the three women.

Jane and Alison looked at the constable with murderous intent but didn't dare move. Annabel lay on the floor, screaming in pain.

Alex managed to struggle to his feet and took the rifle from Arwyn.

"Check on the dog," the hunter instructed. The constable nodded and went over to where the wounded Akita was whining.

Daniel had moved to Sarah's side and was trying to get the lady to respond.

"Untie her and lie her on her back," Alex shouted at Mr

Cooper without moving his eyes from the three women.

"Evans? Where are you?" the chief constable shouted from further down the Edge.

"On the plateau," Arwyn called back. A few minutes later, policemen poured through the trees accompanied by Doctor Hales.

The doctor rushed over to Sarah immediately as Constable Evans explained what had happened to Captain Jonnes Smith.

Daniel didn't leave Sarah's side as the doctor examined her. Alex put down the rifle and went to check on the wounded dog that was now being ignored in the commotion.

The Akita whined and licked Alex's hand as the hunter sat down beside it. The shot had glanced off the side of the dog, so it was bleeding, but it was a graze that wasn't too deep.

The two sat in the forest and watched as Sarah was carried down the Edge by two policemen flanked by the doctor and Daniel.

The three women were handcuffed and led away by the remaining policemen whilst Constable Evans was praised by the chief constable. Eventually Alex and the dog were alone in the forest. The lantern that Alex had been carrying had been broken when he was knocked from his feet, but the lantern that Daniel had been carrying was now sat on the ground on the other side of the fire.

Mr Hunter got up gingerly and kicked earth onto the fire, dowsing the flames, before he picked up the lantern using his bad arm and hefty the injured dog onto his other shoulder.

Chapter 20

When Sarah opened her eyes, she wasn't at Grangeback. A nurse was stood leaning over her shoulder, and Daniel Cooper was sat next to George Webb-Kneelingroach on the other side of her bed.

"Where am I?" Sarah asked groggily.

"The Manchester Royal Infirmary. Doctor Hales had brought you here, after Constable Evans, Alex and Mr Cooper found you," George explained gruffly.

The brigadier was glad that Sarah was alive and finally awake, but he was furious that she had snuck out of the house to search for the missing men on her own and had ended up in the hospital for her trouble.

"What happened?" Sarah asked as she tried to sit up and felt pain shooting through her shoulder.

"You were shot," George replied curtly.

"What happened to Constable Evans and Mr Hunter?" Sarah asked, ignoring the harshness in the brigadier's voice.

"Hunter is at the lodge. The doctor agreed he was well

enough to be allowed to rest at home as long as Cooky took him food, and Mrs Bosworth checked on him every day," Daniel explained.

"Constable Evans returned to his duties, and Mr Taylor has returned home with his fiancée," George said.

"What about the woman?" Sarah said.

"The three women that kidnapped you are in jail, and they won't be leaving it any time soon," Daniel replied.

"That's good," Sarah replied as she closed her eyes and fell asleep.

"You need to let her rest. Come back tomorrow, she should be more awake then," the nurse said.

Daniel and George both stood and left the ward that Sarah was being treated on. Doctor Hales would be there later to check on Sarah, so the brigadier had no qualms about leaving the girl in the hospital on her own.

"Brigadier, can I ask what the relationship between Sarah and Hunter is?" Daniel asked as the two men walked down the hospital corridor.

"What their relationship is?" George frowned.

"Hunter seems to hold her in rather high esteem, and she seems to have a rather high regard for him. Is he one of her suitors?" Mr Cooper asked.

"Not that I am aware of," George replied.

"I see, then, as she is your ward, I intend to court Lady Sarah," Daniel said, with more confidence than he felt.

"Is that so? What will your mother say?" the brigadier asked with a wry smile on his face.

"It doesn't matter. She will be at Tatton Park. I have bought Duffleton Hall. I will be moving there directly," Daniel replied.

"So we're to be neighbours then? That will make Stickleback rather more lively," George answered, "Do you know where Henry is moving to?"

"He is lodging with Miss Baker in the village. He hasn't been living in Duffleton Hall since his son was arrested," Daniel responded.

"If you intend to court Sarah, then I would pay a visit to Mr Hunter when we get back to Stickleback Hollow," George said.

It was three days into November, and things had returned to normality in Stickleback Hollow and at Grangeback. Sarah would be kept in the hospital for another two weeks at the very least. Now that Duffleton Hall had been sold, it wouldn't take long for the news to spread that Daniel Cooper would be moving into the neighbourhood without his mother.

Constable Evans had spent the last few days investigating the break-in at Miss Baker's shop on All Hallows' Eve.

The seamstress was right that only her leather tools were missing, but they hadn't appeared in any of the pawn shops or on any of the more suspect market stalls.

Arwyn hadn't seen Alex since All Hallows' Eve, so the constable took a detour into the woods to visit the lodge.

He found Mr Hunter sat outside the lodge with the wounded Akita sat beside him. The dog seemed to have formed an attachment to the hunter after he had rescued him from the plateau on the Edge.

The dog raised its head and growled when it saw Arwyn approaching, but the Welshman was saved from being mauled by Alex placing a reassuring hand on the scruff of the dog's neck.

"Easy Pattinson," the hunter said in a gentle voice. The dog stopped growling and put his head back down on its paws.

"I wouldn't have thought that you would have made friends with it after what happened to your shoulder," Constable Evans said as he stopped a little further away than he normally would have.

"He was just following orders. Can't hold that against him," Alex replied as he patted the head of the dog, "You look like you have something serious on your mind."

"I do, can we talk inside?" Arwyn asked.

Alex stood up and opened the door to the lodge. Pattinson and Constable Evans both followed him indoors. Pattinson padded over to the fireside and lay down as Alex lit the logs in the grate and Arwyn sat down in one of the armchairs.

"What's worrying you?" Mr Hunter asked as the fire crackled to life, and Alex sat down in one of the other chairs.

"Why would anyone steal leather tools from Miss Baker?" the constable asked.

"I don't know. Why would someone think that Sarah knew anything about the opium industry?" Alex replied.

"Do you think Stuart Moore was involved with everything that happened that night?" Arwyn asked.

"Because his sister was one of the women involved?

150

No, I don't," Alex said.

"You sound pretty sure," Arwyn looked at Alex with a confused expression.

"I am. I went to see Harry yesterday; to ask him about Jane Beech," Alex began to explain.

"And?" Arwyn creased his brow.

"He wasn't at the family home. According to his parents, he hasn't lived there for nearly two years. He's been working for the East India Company," Mr Hunter continued.

"So, what does that mean?" the constable asked.

"I checked with Wilbraham, Harry doesn't have any connection to the East India Company. He's been working for Lord Joshua St. Vincent and his brother, Callum," Alex said with a sigh.

"Then why do his parents think he is working for the East India Company?" Arwyn asked.

"It is easier to tell your family that you work for a reputable business instead of a pair of greedy brothers," Alex shrugged.

"What does all of this have to do with Lady Sarah?" Arwyn asked, shaking his head.

"Lord and Mr St. Vincent work for Lady de

Mandeville. She's the one that sent Lieutenant Forsythe after the pocket watch. She's John Smith. She has been using agents to import opium into China, and then her merchants within the country have been selling it to the people there. She has been making a fortune out of the practice that no other power in Europe can match," Alex said as he stared at the fire.

"And the reason she wants the pocket watch back is the same reason that Lady Sarah was being asked about poppies?" Arwyn said slowly.

"It seems that way. Lord and Mr St. Vincent are currently in Japan looking after some business interests there, but there was an announcement in the times a few weeks ago, Lord Joshua St. Vincent was engaged to Miss Annabel Turner," Alex replied.

"What do you mean, was?" Arwyn frowned.

"After failing to kill Sarah and get the pocket watch, and managing to get arrested instead, do you think that Lord Joshua St. Vincent can be associated with a woman like that?" Alex sighed.

"No, I see what you mean. Why would three women be sent to ask Sarah questions about poppies?" Arwyn asked, shaking his head.

"Women can infiltrate high society much more easily than men can. It is easier for them to befriend a young woman or even remove men that are protecting her without arousing any suspicion," Alex replied.

"Do you think the missing leather tools have anything to do with this?" Arwyn asked.

"Maybe, until they appear again, who can say? But I am certain that Lady de Mandeville isn't going to give up."

Lord Joshua St. Vincent had been waiting in the city of Chester for five days. He had arrived on 30th October and brought three women with him from the Orient. He was staying at the Blossoms Hotel, waiting for the three women to return with good news. He had expected the women to return two days ago, and his patience was exhausted from waiting.

He had brought these three women to accomplish this task because he believed he could trust them. They were women that he had seduced and that had proven their loyalty to him and his bed by assassinating a variety of different targets that stood in his way, and the way of his employer.

He had sent a letter to the chief constable, requesting that the women be released into his custody, but no reply had come.

Instead he had received a note that read:

Most unsatisfactory

J.S.

There was little that he could do at present, but wait for word from the chief constable about whether the women would be released or not. If they were to be kept in jail, then they would need to be eliminated. Ideally, the women would be returned to him. He could question them about what they had learned and what had happened on All Hallows' Eve, enjoy the pleasure of their company one final time and have them removed from his life for their failure.

There were plenty of ways that women could be removed without killing them. Joshua's preferred method was mental asylums as women could be incarcerated for a number of reasons, none of which needed to be proved when the woman was delivered to the asylum.

In a mental asylum, no one would listen to a word the women had to say on any subject, and he would be saved the inconvenience of a most undesirable marriage.

Lord St. Vincent was a man of ambition, and it didn't matter who he had to step on in order to reach his goals.

A knock at the door heralded the arrival of a response from the chief constable. Miss Turner was to be released into Joshua's custody, but Miss Beech and Miss Moore were both too ill to be released. They had become ill with a strange fever that had come on very suddenly. It had taken less than a day to rob them of their strength, and now they were both confined to their beds.

Joshua went to collect Annabel from the police house and brought her back to the Blossom hotel.

"I hear that Alison and Jane are sick," Joshua said as he sat down on one of the large sofas.

"I was told that if we failed, they were to be eliminated," Annabel replied.

"I see, then you poisoned them?" Joshua asked.

"Her ladyship provided me with a very toxic and exotic poison that has proven to be very effective in the past," Annabel smiled.

"She will be pleased that it was used to such good effect," Lord St. Vincent said as he leaned back and thought to himself.

Miss Turner believed that she was safe from the wrath of Lady de Mandeville because she had dispatched the other two women as penance for her failure. Joshua knew that was not the case, but it would take a few days for news of Miss Beech and Miss Moore being taken ill to reach the duchess.

When it did, then she would send instructions to Joshua to get rid of Miss Turner, but until then he would have his fun and let the girl think that in the dangerous world of deception and politics, she was safe from retribution.

~*~*~

Love this book? Need to get the next one today?

Lady Sarah is in grave danger, with more than just her life at risk. After all, there are some fates that are worse than death.

Mr Daniel Cooper of Stickleback Hollow, Book 3 in the Mysteries of Stickleback Hollow is waiting for you now.

~*~*~

Looking for more than just books? You can get the latest releases from me, signed paperbacks and hardbacks, mugs, t-shirts, journals and much more from my Read Round the Clock Shopify store.

~*~*~

Want to help a reader out? Review are crucial when it comes to helping readers choose their next book and you can help them by leaving just a few sentences about this book as a review. It doesn't have to be anything fancy, just what you liked about the book and who you think might like to read it.

Use the QR below to leave a review.

If you don't have time to leave a review or don't feel confident writing one, recommending a book to your family, friends and co-workers can help them choose their next book, so feel free to spread the word.

Historical Note

Wilbraham and Elizabeth Egerton were the couple in residence at Tatton Park in 1838. Wilbraham became the owner of Tatton Park in 1806, when his father. William Egerton died. William Egerton was originally called William Tatton, but his name was legally changed in 1780 when his mother, Hester, became the heiress to the Tatton Estates. Hester Tatton nee Egerton was the sister of Samuel Egerton who left Tatton Park after his wife and daughter both died. Wilbraham Egerton and Elizabeth Egerton nee Sykes had three daughters and seven sons.

William, Thomas, Edward and Charles were all alive when this book is set. Sadly Mark Egerton died at the age of 16 in 1831, and George Egerton died in the first year of his life in 1814. There are almost no records that I was able to find to help with the character of Charlotte Egerton. There isn't even a year of birth in many records, so I made her into the twin of Charles as Charlotte is the female form of Charles. The other two daughters of Wilbraham and Elizabeth were named after their mother, and both died in the first year of their lives. The first Elizabeth died in 1811 and the second Elizabeth died in 1821.

In terms of their partners in life, William married Charlotte Loftus, Wilbraham never married but died in 1841, Thomas married Charlotte Milner, Edward married Mary Pierrepont, and Charles married Margaret Cust.

All Hallows' Eve was not the occasion for trick or treating in the Victorian age. Originally it was a time of the world of the living and dead being closer together than at any other point in the year. The veil between the two was thought to be drawn back so that the dead could once again return to the world of the living.

Then it became All Saint's Day when the saints and martyrs were honoured instead of ghosts and ghouls. Food was left out for the hungry and the homeless, but there was still the superstition that the dead and things that go bump in the night might be lurking about.

In 1838 there was no Who's Who, it wasn't published until 1849, and there were no listings such as the society pages. There would have been no instant record that people could have gone to study in order to discover Sarah's name. So instead there was gossip. One person writing to a well-connected friend in London society would have been able to find out almost anything about Sarah from her aunts and cousins, and then they would be free to share what they discovered. Gossip and scandal did and still do a good deal of damage to the reputation of an individual without any proof being required.

Countess Szonja and the Hungarian Prince are both fictions. However, the flood that occurred in Pest is not. On 13th March 1838, the city was flooded with some parts of the city being covered with eight feet of water. Two-thirds of the buildings in the city were damaged or destroyed, and 150 people lost their lives. Many European nations came to Hungary's aid to help stop famine and disease from spreading across the continent. The flooding of the Danube is thought to have been caused by a combination of melting snow and heavy rain. In

1873 Pest merged with the cities of Buda and Obuda to become the current capital of Hungary, Budapest. The character of Countess Szonja was named after a friend of the same name who hails from the city.

The mention of Charles Dickens serial in the Spectator refers to Nicholas Nickleby. On 31st March 1838, the first of twenty parts of the serial was published in the London magazine, the final part wasn't published until 29th October 1839. Nicholas Nickleby is a book designed to expose the terrible state of Yorkshire Boarding schools. Dickens and his illustrator, Hablot Browne, visited Bowes Academy in Yorkshire where he got the idea for Nicholas Nickleby. In 1823 Bowes Academy had been prosecuted for neglect after two pupils became blind after continual beatings and malnutrition. After the investigation, things did improve at the school, but it was still commonplace for a pupil to die every year.

The SS Great Western was designed by Isambard Kingdom Brunel and did make the journey to New York from Avonmouth in 15 days between 8th April and 23rd April 1838.

On 28th June 1838 in Westminster Abbey the Coronation of Queen Victoria took place thought she had been queen since 20th June 1837.

The Boat Race between Oxford and Cambridge was first held in 1829, but it wasn't until 1856 that it became an annual event, though this was suspended during the First and Second World Wars. Since it was introduced there has only been one draw. Oxford has won the boat race 79 times and Cambridge 82 (these figures are correct as of 16th March 2017). The second boat race was held in 1836. The dead heat between the two universities occurred in 1877 when both teams finished the course in 24 minutes and 8 seconds in bad weather, though the idea it was actually a dead heat is disputed when the announcement is said to have been "Dead heat...to Oxford by six feet". There have also been two attempted mutinies by Oxford, one in 1959 and one in 1987. The argument that Richard and Gordon have about where the boat race should be held is the contestation that occurred at the time with Oxford preferring Henley and Cambridge preferring London.

Stickleback Edge is based on Alderly Edge in Cheshire. The

Edge is a rather steep hill that has adders living on one side of it and some rather enjoyable walks on the other side of it. The Edge is a site of druid magic and also has a local legend that tells of a wizard looking for a horse for one of 140 knights dressed in silver armour that are sleeping under the Edge, waiting to fight the last battle of the world. The legend is emblazoned in a pictorial façade on the side of Sainsbury's in Wilmslow.

On the subject of wolves, though the official records state that the last wolf in the United Kingdom was killed in 1680 in Perthshire by Sir Ewen Cameron of Lochiel, however, people reported seeing wild wolves in Scotland up until 1888. Though the inhabitants of Stickleback Hollow would not have spent their lives living in fear of wolves descending in rabid hunting packs to carry off children in the depths of especially cruel winters, there is a primal fear that is associated with wolves that is something that we can relate to even now.

The idea of being hunted by a large beast that is smart, strong and fast is terrifying enough, but a pack of them coming down in the dead of night to claim the lives of loved ones is enough to give the bravest soul cause to pause.

There are many theories as to why wolves, in particular, can create so much terror in humans that have never even seen one before, but for the sake of this book, I chose to observe the ideas that Jack London outlines in *The Call of the Wild*, that it is something of our ancestors in our souls. The ancient terror from when time first began that has become buried by civilisation, but in moments of life or death, the veil of society is ripped away, and the instincts of ages past come to the surface to help us survive. Though this isn't strictly a historical note, it is something I thought was worth explaining, if only to mention the work of Jack London (he also wrote *White Fang*).

It is also worth mentioning that my surname means wood of wolves (depending on the translation, it can be one of many variations of "of wolves")

The Baker rifle came into existence in 1799 and is the rifle that was used by the green jackets in the British Army during the Napoleonic War (and yes, it is the rifle carried by one Mr Richard Sharpe). It was issued to the British army until around

165

1841, which is three years after the rifle production had finished. There were several different variations of the rifle, which included a shorter carbine version for cavalry.

Papaver somniferum is the Latin name for the poppies that poppy seeds, poppy seed oil and opium both come from. The seed pods from this particular poppy were used to create tinctures such as laudanum and other opiates. The pods are cut, and the latex that comes from the green seed pods is allowed to dry before it is collected. This is where we get opium from (not the seeds themselves as many people think).

The first opium war between China and the British East India Company began in 1839 on 18th March and lasted for 3 years, 5 months, 1 week and 4 days. It was during this war that Hong Kong Island became part of the British territories. The British won the war. The war began because China was largely self-sufficient at the time and though traded tea and silks with the Western world, there was virtually no exportation from the west into China.

The East India Company began to auction opium that had

been grown on large plantations in India to independent foreign traders who then sold it to traders on the Chinese coast, who took the opium into the Chinese interior. This reversed the flow of European silver and created a large number of opium addicts in China that alarmed officials. The Daoguang Emperor rejected proposals to legalise and tax opium in 1839 and tried to solve the problem by abolishing the trade and appointing Viceroy Lin Zexu. It is during this war that the British used its gunnery and naval power to ensure the defeat of the Chinese and led to the coining of the phrase, gunboat diplomacy.

Shinobi or ninja were mercenaries and spies during the Sengoku period, but after the unification of Japan in the 17th century, the shinobi disappeared. In the 17th and 18th century, there were shinobi manuals that were written, often based on the philosophy of the Chinese military. By the 1800s, the ninja had become a figure of mystery and folklore that had abilities to become invisible, walk on water, shapeshift, summon animals, create copies of themselves and even control the elements.

Handcuffs that were used before 1862 were a one size fits all type of contraption. In 1862 the ratchet design of handcuffs, which we would recognise as being the basis of modern handcuffs, was patented.

When it comes to women being committed to mental asylums in the 19th Century, don't believe all the claims made on the internet. Women were committed for diseases such as dementia, acute mania, melancholia and acute mania, along with intemperance, ill health, traumatic injury and masturbation. These were as true for men as they were for women though. The list of reasons for admission that you may have seen circulating on the internet are some of the supposed symptoms of the above conditions, not the reasons they were admitted. However, it was still very easy for husbands to have wives committed, or in Lord St. Vincent's case, an unwanted fiancée.

The East India Company still exists. It made a fortune trading luxury goods and opium out of India. Today it is still an importer of luxury goods which include tea and silver. They are often painted as villains in popular culture. However, I have tried to avoid such a bias as it is extraordinarily easy to colour history to how we wish it to appear (I also really like their tea).

About the Series

Mysteries abound

When her parents die from fever, Lady Sarah Montgomery Baird Watson-Wentworth has to leave India, a land she was born and raised in, and travel to England for the first time. Finding it almost impossible to adjust to London society, Sarah flees to the county of Cheshire and the country estate of Grangeback that borders the village of Stickleback Hollow.

A place filled with oddballs, eccentrics and more suspicious characters than you can shake a stick at, Sarah feels more at home in the sleepy little village than she ever did in the big city, however, even sleepy little villages have mysteries that must be solved.

Set in Victorian England, the Mysteries of Stickleback Hollow follows the crime solving efforts of Constable Arwyn Evans, Mr. Alexander Hunter and Lady Sarah Montgomery Baird Watson-Wentworth.

From theft to murder, supernatural occurrences and missing people, Stickleback Hollow is a magical place filled with oddballs, outcasts, rogues, eccentrics and ragamuffins.

Preview from the next book
Mr Daniel Cooper of Stickleback Hollow

There was something about him that she didn't like; something in his mannerisms made her feel uncomfortable in his presence. This, coupled with the warnings from Grace and Lady Szonja, were enough to make Sarah want to make this particular meeting as brief as possible.

"I do, walk with me and I shall reveal all," the young lord grinned at Sarah and offered her his arm.

Sarah paused for a moment to think before she accepted the offered arm and allowed Joshua to walk.

"Where are we going?" Sarah asked as Lord St. Vincent escorted her down the street to a carriage and insisted that she board.

"I am taking you to Miss Turner. She is in a hospital in Bache. I am sure she will be very glad of a visit," Joshua replied as he pushed Sarah into the carriage and followed quickly after her.

The carriage lurched forward and trundled out of the city. It was already dark, so no one had seen Sarah being pushed into the carriage on the dimly lit street. No one paid any attention to the carriage as it made its way from the city and out to Bache Hall.

Eventually, the carriage came to a halt outside a grand looking building. Standing outside was a woman with three large looking men.

"What is this place?" Sarah frowned as the woman opened the carriage door.

"Good evening, my lord. Is this the young lady?" the woman said.

"Good evening, Mrs Bird. It is indeed," Joshua smiled nastily at Sarah.

"What's going on?" Sarah demanded.

"Quiet now, girl. Take her inside," the matron ordered the three large men.

"No! What do you think you are doing! Get your hands off me!" Sarah screamed as she tried to push the men back from the carriage door.

Lord St. Vincent watched the altercation for a few moments with amusement before he intervened. He grabbed Sarah by the hair and pulled back her head so he could whisper in her ear.

"This is the Cheshire County Lunatic Asylum. I'm sorry that things ended in this fashion, but my employer needs you out of the way, and a piece of their property returned. You understand. I was hoping that you would be a much more amenable prospect; it would have been so much more enjoyable to see you join with us than this alternative. But it can't be helped. Such devotion to a mere groundskeeper is not a desirable trait for my line of work; so you see, this was really all that I could do – short of killing you of course," Joshua hissed in her ear before he pushed her forcefully out of the carriage and into the waiting arms of the three men.

"Thank you, my lord. We'll see she gets the very best of care," Mrs Bird said with a curtesy.

"I appreciate your help and your discretion, Mrs Bird. You understand the embarrassment, this is my sister," Lord St. Vincent said with a feigned pained expression on his face.

"Of course, my lord, I quite understand. She is listed as Miss Stephanie Hunter in our records to avoid any possible scandal," Mrs Bird replied as Sarah was carried into the hospital, engaged in a futile struggle to escape her captors.

"Thank you, my family will be sure to show it's appreciation for your discretion. If you'll excuse me, I must

175

return to the city, I have a dinner engagement," Lord St. Vincent said, and his carriage lurched away from the hospital leaving Sarah in the hands of the asylum.

Get your copy now!

About the Author

I was born in Macclesfield, Cheshire, UK, and raised in the nearby town of Wilmslow. From an early age I discovered I had a flair and passion for writing.

I began writing at the age of 7 and was first published in 2010. I currently live with my partner, Matt, and our two cats in Christchurch, New Zealand.

As an avid horsewoman and gamer, I also have a passion for singing, dancing, the theatre, and my garden.

Facebook: https://www.facebook.com/AuthorC.S.Woolley

Instagram: https://www.instagram.com/thecswoolley

Website: http://.mightierthanthesworduk.com

Acknowledgements

Writing can be an extremely lonely profession at times, but thankfully I never have to go through any of the pressures alone. My wonderful Matthew has been a source of constant support to me during all of my writing endeavours since we first met. I couldn't ask for a more fitting partner to share my life or love with.

Writing is not something I stumbled into either, my mother, Helen, took me, and my sisters, to the library every weekend when we were young to get different books, and I always maxed out the number of books I could get. Not only did she encourage me to read, but to write as well. To say I have been writing stories and poetry since I was 7 is not an exaggeration and the development of my writing career is due in no small part to her.

My mother-in-law, Lesley, has also been a source of unflinching and unwavering support, something I could not do without.

To Laura and Sam, who have read and offered opinions, death threats and encouragement on my early drafts, you are true treasures. Amy, you too are worth your weight and more in gold for all your love and support.

It may seem that writers only function alone, but I am blessed to be part of an amazing community of authors whom I know that I have helped push me to even greater heights and success. So to Quinn Ward, Donna Higton, Scarlett Braden Moss, Bryan Cohen, Chez Churton, Robert Scanlon, Jen Lassalle, Brittany Weese, Phoebe Ravencroft, and Marcel Liemant, my dear friends, thank you.

And finally, to you, dear reader, without you there would be no books, no series, no career. I want to thank you for all the time that you spend reading my work, reviewing it, sharing it with your friends and family. Without you there would be nothing. Thank you from the bottom of my heart.

Until we meet again in my next book, thank you and adieu.

Made in the USA
Monee, IL
30 September 2024

66861096R00105